Mad about the girl . . .

Chris sat watching them. She was annoyed and, on two glasses of wine, already a little tipsy — annoyed with Johnnie for dancing with the girl, holding her too close and pressing his lips to the top of her head. Annoyed with Carol for enjoying it. And annoyed with herself for not doing something about it.

She could not bear the way Carol relaxed against Johnnie, the way she was dancing with her eyes closed and smiling. They looked good together and it irritated her.

Chris got up and went unsteadily to cut in. She put a hand heavily on Johnnie's shoulder. "Shove off, mate," she said. "I'm not dead yet."

Johnnie released the girl. "Sorry, skipper," he said.

Chris took Carol in her arms and stood holding the girl tight against her. They swayed to the rhythm.

"You don't have to be so nasty," Carol said.

"Look," Chris said angrily, "you're my girl."

CHRIS

~

by
Randy Salem

CHRIS

~

by
Randy Salem

The Naiad Press, Inc.
1989

Printed in the United States of America
First Naiad Press Edition
    Chris first appeared as a paperback original novel published by Beacon Books in 1959 at the beginning of the era referred to as the golden age of lesbian paperback originals.

Cover design by Pat Tong and Bonnie Liss
    (Phoenix Graphics)
Typeset by Sandi Stancil

Library of Congress Cataloging-in-Publication Data

Salem, Randy.
    Chris / by Randy Salem.
        p.   cm.
    ISBN 0-941483-42-8 : $8.95
    I. Title
PS3569.A45935C47   1989
813.54—dc20   89-34017
                                                   CIP

1

Chris took the girl's wrist in her hand and gently moved the arm that had been flung across her chest. She sat up then, careful not to wake the girl, and slid to the edge of the bed. With her toes she groped for the sandals, found one and wiggled a foot into it. Then the other. She braced her feet against the floor.

Now, she knew, she would have to open her eyes. It wasn't easy, that bit. The lids came up slowly, painfully, grating inside her skull like two rusty, ponderous dungeon gates. The eyes came slowly down from somewhere at the back of her head.

"Focus, damn you."

The eyes swam for a moment, then settled. They stared blindly away from the bed, across the room, through a door. There they found an object, caught and held it, and sent back a message.

Chris got it. And moved. She was across the room, through the door and hanging breathless over the john before she had time to realize she couldn't make it.

Then the ugly business of sobering up and getting the hell out of there. Water on the face. Half a dozen aspirin from the medicine cabinet. Into the shower to stand under the freezing needle spray. A brisk rub with a rough towel.

Chris ran through her routine in ten minutes flat. She had it down to a science by now. Every Saturday night for four years, while Dizz went home to be company to her folks, Chris had gone out to a Village bar, gotten stoned and picked up the first girl who came along. When you look like Chris, it's not hard. And every Sunday morning she came to in the dame's apartment, made a bolt for the john, and stepped into the shower. Once there'd been a blonde with a bathtub. Chris had been hung over for three days.

She picked up a comb from the back of the hopper and turned to the mirror. It had seen better days. But then, so had Chris. The business of looking in the mirror was the worst part. Not just the searching for tell-tale signs, the bruises and hickeys of drunken passion, but having to look yourself square in the eye and admit: "You damned jerk. You've done it again."

She looked now, at the too good-looking face, the perfect head with its perfectly waved black hair, the

2

long neck. There was an ugly reddish bruise just under the left ear. Dizz would see it. She wouldn't say anything — she never did. But she would see it and she would suffer.

And the eyes. A dark green. Deep, deep eyes that looked down into the soul of the woman. But such was the nature of the beast that even the soul appeared beautiful. No one but Chris had ever known the depravity of the mind and soul behind those eyes. And Chris found it to her advantage not to tell.

She ran the comb quickly through her hair, took a long drink of water, and walked back to the other room. She did not glance at the bed. Her slacks, shirt and jacket were hung on the back of a chair, neatly, and her underwear on the end of the bed. She hadn't been that careful, she knew. But she appreciated the creases in her slacks.

She stood dressed in front of a full-length mirror and liked what she saw. Lean and firm, built like a young boy, she did not look like a thirty-year-old woman. She was all things beautiful, graceful and desirable. A pet to be doted upon and spoiled. The thought amused her and she smiled.

"Chris?"

She turned toward the bed and realized that the girl had been watching her. She had forgotten the girl already, as she forgot them all. She had never known her name. That helped.

"Yes?"

Chris walked over to the bed and stood beside it, looking down at the girl. She saw that the girl was extremely attractive, a dark brunette with a pert nose and sleepy eyes. Last night she had had two heads and not much of a face.

"Chris, may I see you again?" The voice was soft, wispy. It could make a person feel loved, that voice. So could the hands. One of them reached out to Chris and she took it and pressed her lips to the palm.

"No," Chris said. "I'm afraid that's not possible. I've got a girl. I live with her."

"I know. Or at least I guessed. You kept calling me Dizz last night." The girl smiled at Chris, her eyes tender. "Did you two have a fight or how come she let you out of her sight?"

Chris hesitated. The truth was nobody's business. "No. No fight." She did not know how to explain without telling her everything.

"Look, Chris," the girl said. "I don't mean to be nosey. But I like you enough to care." She withdrew her hand from Chris' fingers, pulled herself up in the bed and leaned back against the pillows. "I would like to see you again. I know you're in love with somebody. But thought maybe, since you were out last night, you could get out again." She grinned at her own thoughts. "And as far as having a girl is concerned, we could just be pals, if you'd like."

Chris wrinkled her nose, then laughed quietly. "Honey, I might just do that. As a matter of fact, I'm free every Saturday night."

"Good," the girl said. "Now do me a favor. There's paper and a pencil on the desk. Copy down my phone number." She pointed to the desk.

Chris walked to the desk, picked up a pencil and tore a sheet from a small dime store pad. She glanced for a second at the telephone, then scribbled down a Yukon number. She turned and looked at the girl.

"Honey," Chris said. "Just one more thing."

4

"Yes, what is it?"

"Honey, I'm embarrassed." She wasn't. She never was. But the girl saw embarrassment on her face. "But tell me, what's your name?"

The girl tossed her hair back from her shoulders and a laugh sounded deep in her throat. "Carol," she said. "Carol Martin."

Chris came to the bed, leaned one knee on it and cupped Carol's chin in her hands. "Pleased to meet you, darling." She smiled and bent her head to meet the girl's lips. It was a long kiss, full of the promise of many to come. "I'm Chris Hamilton. Christopher, that is."

"Yes, I know," Carol said. "Prophetic, wasn't it?"

Chris like this girl. Somehow, she knew, they spoke the same language. A civilized patter just padded enough to hide the rusty razor underneath. They would both wield that razor to cut the legs off anybody in reach. But not each other. They wouldn't hurt each other. They might very well destroy each other completely, but it wouldn't hurt.

Carol continued. "I also know you're a writer. Articles. And that you're the top conchologist, an amateur marine biologist and an expert swimmer. I know when and where you were born and where you went to school. And, as of last night, I even know you have a large mole on your rear end."

Chris felt vaguely uncomfortable. She preferred to be one up on the world. She did not behave well when backed into a corner. Sometimes she kicked. More often she simply slithered away.

"I also have a diamond-shaped birthmark on the back of my right hand and a cavity in a back molar,"

Chris said. She paused to take a pack of cigarettes from her jacket pocket. "Or did you notice?"

She shook the pack and flipped up a cigarette. "Want one?" she asked, extending it toward Carol.

"No thanks," Carol said. "Not before breakfast."

Chris picked the cigarette from the pack with her lips and brought the small gold lighter from her pocket. She inhaled deeply and blew a puff of smoke toward the ceiling.

"I always have aspirin for breakfast," Chris said. "But please explain yourself. How come you know these little tidbits about me? I think I was much too high to tell you myself." She never told the facts anyhow, drunk or not. But it sounded better this way.

She knew Carol was aware of her discomfort. And obviously she enjoyed it. There was something infinitely satisfying about this game. The business of watching Chris squirm, her whole being searching into corners for a way out while that beautiful face remained a mask, the placid surface of a silent pool.

"Simple," Carol said, splaying her fingers on the sheet. "I'm Dr. Brandt's new assistant. I saw you down at the museum one day and he told me who you were. So I looked up the file they've got on you. It didn't mention the mole. That I saw for myself." She winked at Chris. "Like I said, simple."

Chris took time to breathe. "Okay, I'll buy that." She took a deep drag on the cigarette. "How come Brandt's got a woman assistant, though? I thought he specialized in precious young men."

"So I've heard," Carol said. "I just happened to be on the loose when this job opened up. I know my business. He hired me." She yawned and slid down further beneath the blankets. "My first assignment is to sort out and classify that batch of stuff you brought back from Key West." She grinned impishly. "And frankly, if I hadn't found you in the bar last night, I had planned to use that as an in."

Chris meticulously snubbed out the cigarette in a tiny copper tray. She took two steps and slowly set the tray on the bookcase beside the bed. She took two steps back to face the girl. Then she said, with studied nonchalance, "Oh?"

Carol pushed back the covers, sat up and swung her legs over the edge of the bed. "Chris," she said in that I-can-make-you-happy voice, "I don't know how to be coy. I quit trying when I was twelve and broke a little boy's nose because he tried to kiss me. When I want something, I make no bones. And I want you."

"You like the mole."

"Hmm. Partially that," Carol said. "And partially because I like your work. I've been reading your stuff for years, you know. At first because it was my field. Then just because it appealed to me." She was warming to her topic, speaking earnestly. "You write about the sea like others write about a first love, with the same tenderness and doting devotion. What anybody else would make a dull, dry treatise, you render into an elegy." She paused for just a second. "Not that I don't know better than to judge you by what you write."

"I hope so," Chris said. "I'm a disagreeable bitch. I'm snide and sarcastic and sometimes cruel. A lecher and a drunkard to boot."

Chris knew these things were true. But before Dizz happened, they hadn't been like that. She used

7

to pet dogs and help old ladies across the street. But that was four years ago. And in those four years, every decent instinct she'd ever had had been strangled in the unrelenting grip of frustration and self-pity.

"Chris," a tiny voice cut into her reverie. "Chris, listen to me and stop looking at shadows. I know what you think of yourself and I imagine there are probably good reasons for it. Most of the time I might even agree, since you work so hard at creating that impression."

Chris fumbled for another cigarette. She could not look into the affectionately accusing eyes. She fished one out of the pack and lit it.

"But, darling," Carol continued, her voice low. "I know a couple of things you don't. I know that you write like an angel. And I know you can be a tender lover even when you're drunk." She laughed with delight. "And that at the moment you've got shiny pink earlobes."

Chris abruptly turned her back and walked to the window. She hadn't realized where she was but she looked down now to the street and recognized First Avenue. Probably the Seventies. Dirty, ugly neighborhood. Across the street a box of twenty-five cent books sat in front of an antique shop. A mongrel with yellow splotches stopped to sniff and lift a leg. A fat guy in an undershirt came out of the shop and yelled. The dog raised his head and then, with infinite boredom, he turned away to finish his business in peace. The fat guy just stood there, his hands on his hips, too exasperated to find the words.

Dizz would have laughed. She would have laughed harder if he'd turned around and aimed at the guy.

Chris flipped the cigarette into the street.

She heard Carol patter barefoot across the room behind her. She turned and looked down at the girl. She was naked and she was tiny and she looked soft and like it would feel good to hold her.

"Chris," she said, "don't be angry. Please." She pouted, but playfully. She reached up and touched the bruise and let her fingers trail lightly down Chris' neck and under the collar. "Darling, kiss me."

Chris put her arms around the girl and let her hands trace the curve of her back. She put one hand on Carol's back and pulled her tight. Her lips sought Carol's ear and she nipped at the lobe. Her tongue probed into the ear, touched lightly the downy hairs on the neck.

"Darling," Carol breathed. "Oh please, darling."

Chris carried the girl to the bed and put her down gently on the sheet. She bent across her and met the girl's hungry lips with her own. "Baby, I can't," she whispered. "I've got to leave. Now."

Dizz will be waiting. Dizz will be waiting.

But Chris felt the flame of desire quiver up her spine. Her hand moved over the girl's flesh and she heard the moan of mounting ecstasy. Her ears were pounding and her heart. Her mouth closed on Carol's and her tongue dug deep.

Dizz is waiting. Dizz is waiting.

"I love you. I love you," Carol crooned. "Darling, take me. Please take me."

All sense of time and of guilt faded before that plea. Chris could not stop now. She was caught in the web of her passion and she took the girl eagerly. She wanted her, wanted her as she had never wanted anything.

Carol sighed and leaned back against the pillows. Her eyes were soft with fulfillment. "I'll take that cigarette now," she said.

Chris lit one and handed it to her. "I've got to go, honey. But I'll be back. We've got a lot of things to talk about."

She left then. Quickly. It was late. Dizz would be waiting. Time enough later to think about Carol.

And Chris knew Carol would take thinking about.

2

Chris paid the cabbie at the corner of Second Avenue and Fiftieth and turned east toward Beekman Place. She needed the block and a half walk to calm down, to get her head in order before she faced Dizz. For a reason she didn't dare comprehend, she had the shakes.

She dug out the cigarettes and pulled one from the pack. Her hands were trembling. She'd lit cigarettes by now everywhere but underwater, but this one took three tries. When it was lit she didn't want it and threw it into the gutter.

She pressed the buzzer for 1R, waited a long minute and got no answer. Her watch showed three-fifteen. Dizz came through that door every Sunday at two, give or take a couple of minutes.

Maybe she's in the john taking a shower or something. Or something. She could be polluted and out cold. No novelty that.

She pulled the keys from the pocket of her slacks and aimed one in the direction of the lock. It connected and turned. She made the hall in three strides and on the fourth got the door of the apartment open and was inside.

The curtains were drawn. It was dark. It was cold and unfriendly.

"Dizz?" The word croaked out and fell flat. She knew Dizz would not answer. Dizz was not there.

She reached a hand over her shoulder and flicked on the kitchen light. She walked into the living room, through to the bedrooms and to the bath beyond, out onto the terrace. She turned on every light in the house.

Then she lit a cigarette.

Frightened now, she crept into the living room and sank ponderously down on the couch. She felt herself turning pea green and the alcohol and the girl and the fear choked and burned in her throat. She wanted to throw up but she could not move.

"She left me," she said to herself. "Just like that. Not a word. She left me, just like that. She left me." Round and round, without sense or meaning, round and round.

Chris did not move or breathe until the cigarette had burned down to her fingers. She moved then, and breathed. She got up and walked to the kitchen and turned on the spigot and doused the cigarette. She let the cold water run on the burn and slapped some of it on her face. She turned off the water and walked back to the couch. Then she began to think.

By some devious means, Chris arrived at the inevitable conclusion — the only love of her life, the only good and perfect thing she had ever known had run out on her. She'd picked up and left her, without a word, without waiting for an explanation.

No good bitch. No good goddamn slut. No good —

Chris realized that she was crying. Sniveling. Her nose, her eyes, her mouth, all of her was crying. And the awareness of this final indignity did not stop the flow. She let loose with all the misery in her and some that she didn't know she had.

The buzzer rang. She heard it, she imagined it. She dreamed it.

Suddenly there was Dizz. Her perfume, her golden hair, her ice blue eyes, her pussy cat smile. Dizz who had left her. And she was laughing and talking. Something about her brother, Roger, and a train. Something about a party. Something about —

"Chris, what's the matter with you? Darling, are you drunk? Why didn't you answer the door? Come meet George. He and Roger went to school together. He drove me home. Have you been crying? Here, blow your nose." She stopped long enough to open her bag and take out a handkerchief. She handed it to Chris, frowning on her the while with stern disapproval.

Chris looked helplessly into the icy eyes, then turned her head away and blew furiously. She looked back. Dizz was studying her disgustedly, as though she were a cockroach in somebody else's apartment.

Chris sighed and relaxed against the cushion. How

13

could she tell Dizz? How could she tell her she loved her? That she cried because she loved her? You just didn't tell Dizz things like that.

The deep, beautiful voice went on as though it had never stopped. "Darling, for heaven's sake, pull yourself together. We've got company."

Of this fact Chris had already become aware. Her eyes had traced a slow straight line from the polished tip of a shoe up to the thin dark face of a handsome young man. The eyes were laughing at her. They meant to be friendly.

Chris did not like this young man. She had never met one she did like, in fact. She sometimes dreamed of finding a cure for them, like for polio. But most especially she did not like this one. She knew instinctively that a mother would simper and pat her hair and consider him an ideal catch for a daughter. His nails were clean and his clothes were tailored to fit. He would have money and a car.

She looked from the young man back to Dizz. With discomfort so terrible that she could grab it in her hands, Chris watched her beloved turn to the young man, smile and reach up to smooth back her hair.

"Darling," Dizz breathed, "this is George Randolph." She said it like he was one of the Elgin marbles. She said it like there'd never been anybody around before he happened.

Then she turned to Chris. "Christopher Hamilton," she said crisply.

Dizz was at her best like this. The nerve center of a social situation, enthralling the mob. And in essence apologizing for the existence of Chris, her idiot child.

Chris did what was expected of her. She rose

14

pointedly to the peak of her five-ten and extended her hand.

George took it and shook vigorously, the way Chris hated.

"This is a real pleasure," he said. He beamed at her like he almost meant it.

"I'm glad to know you," Chris answered. She wasn't, but obviously Dizz wanted her to be.

"George is a lawyer," Dizz said. "A highly successful one, I hear."

George remained modestly silent.

Chris just remained silent.

"Would you like a drink, George?" Dizz asked. "Or maybe some coffee?"

"I can't, Sheila," he said. "Much as I'd like to. I promised Mother I'd take her out to dinner tonight." He adjusted his tie. "I try to see her at least once a week," he grinned. "I'm the baby, you know, and she misses me."

"I'm sorry you have to go," Chris said, relieved and all of a sudden amiable. "I hope we'll be seeing you again." Some day she'd have her tongue cut out for lies like that.

"Oh, yes. You will," he replied. "I promise to make a nuisance of myself. Sheila's a delight and from what she's told me of you, I expect I'll find you the same."

Chris stole a quick look at Dizz. Dizz was paying her no heed at all. She was absorbed in enchanting this creature.

Together they walked with George to the door. Together they said their goodbyes.

Dizz closed the door and turned on her.

"Would you mind, darling, explaining the little

15

performance you put on for us?" Her voice was cold, her eyes bright with contempt.

Chris sighed and walked back to the living room. She stood looking through the French doors to the terrace. The late afternoon sun threw long shadows across the bricks. It was getting chilly with the oncoming of evening. She remembered that September was already half over. She should be getting out in the garden and bedding it down for the winter.

"Chris, don't stand there like a fool. I asked you a question."

"I heard you," Chris said. She walked across to the French doors and pulled them closed. She tugged the cord on the drapes, then reached down to unfasten one where it had caught against a stool.

"Well?" Dizz was becoming overtly impatient. In a minute she would be angry. Then she would take a drink.

Chris moved to a leather sling and sat into it. She took out a cigarette and sat turning it end over end in her fingers. She did not look at Dizz.

"Will he?" she said.

"Will he what?" Dizz answered.

"Make a nuisance of himself?"

"Chris," Dizz began. "I want you to understand something. I like George. I like him very much. And if he wants to see me, I'm going to see him." She crossed to the chair and stood glaring down at Chris. "You know how bored I am here. You're always busy writing or something. We hardly ever go out. I need somebody who's fun for a change."

"Dizz," Chris said, "you know you're free to do as you please. You told me that four years ago."

"Then what's the matter with you?"

16

"I just like to know where I stand. I don't feel that George is vital to my happiness. But I occasionally suffer the delusion that you are." She still did not look at Dizz.

"Darling, you're jealous," Dizz announced. She said it with delight, as though it offered a moment's diversion."

"I haven't decided about that yet," Chris said. "Right now I'm simply annoyed."

"Silly darling," Dizz laughed. She bent down before Chris and laid her cheek against the girl's knee. "My silly darling."

Chris did not move to lay a hand on the proffered head. She took out the lighter and lit the cigarette.

Dizz sat back on the rug and hugged her knees close to her breasts. Chris looked at her and wanted to cry. She always wanted to cry when she looked at Dizz. Dizz with her angel's face and the delicious mouth that curved up at the corners in a perpetual smile. Dizz whose eyes promised everything. Dizz who did not know the meaning of love.

"Honey," Dizz said coyly, "you know I'm yours. I'm not going to fall for George. I just want to have a little fun." She put her hands behind her on the carpet and leaned back. "Besides, he knows all about us. I told him."

"And what, precisely," Chris asked, "is there to know?"

"Darling, don't be vulgar. I told him that we've been living together and that we love each other. He understands. He's been around."

"He understands? He understands what?" Chris asked.

"That I'm not available."

17

"He's a whole man, complete with the usual equipment?"

"Of course."

"Then he doesn't understand," Chris said. "There's never been a man who didn't believe he could take a girl away from another woman. Why should he be different?"

Dizz picked herself up from the floor and started toward the kitchen. She turned at the door and faced Chris. "You give me a pain sometimes. Just because all you think about is sex doesn't make it universal." She went on into the kitchen. "Dinner will be ready in an hour."

Chris knew she had been dismissed. She stubbed out her cigarette in the ashtray beside her and pulled herself out of the chair. She crossed to the bedroom on the left and went in. She shut the door quietly, then flopped down on the bed.

With her hands folded behind her head and her legs stretched up the wall, Chris found a crack in the plaster and focused her attention on it. She wanted to take an ax and hack away at it, beat at it. She wanted to hurt and destroy.

If that bastard lays a hand on Dizz —

She thought back to the night she had met Sheila Elizabeth Dizendorf. It was at a party especially arranged for the purpose by mutual friends. Somebody had decided that it was only right that these two most beautiful of God's creatures should meet. And mate. She had stood for fifteen minutes just looking at the girl, memorizing the lines. Dizz was the most everything woman she had ever seen. She still was. And Chris had been making a careful survey of the field for fifteen years.

18

It was not a question of falling in love. Chris had been in love with Dizz all her life. Dizz was, in one gorgeous package, all her dreams and aspirations. Dizz was it.

Chris never recovered from that initial shock. She knew only one thing: that she wanted this woman to be hers. She would love her and cherish her and slave for her.

"I'm going up to Nova Scotia for a month," Chris had said. "They're after the Oak Island treasure again and I'm out to do an article about it."

"Oh yes. That's the one where there's supposed to be a couple of million pounds under water, isn't it?"

"Right. I want to see for myself. Would you like to come along?"

"Yes, Chris. I would love to," Dizz had smiled. Chris had called her Dizz from the start. She'd thought it was cute at the time. Now it just sounded ironic.

So they went to Nova Scotia. Chris remembered with a poignant ache their first night together. She had gone to Dizz with the simplicity of an adolescent in love, wanting only to make her woman happy, not knowing that from her happiness could come misery and pain. She felt again the dizzy sweetness of the moment, the mounting desire and the headlong fury with which she sped to her doom.

And Dizz. The way she had lain unfulfilled in her arms, moaning a little in her anguish. Then turning away from her to stare blankly at the wall.

Chris recalled vividly her own horror, her feeling of impotence and shame. She had lain there trembling in the dark, very alone. She had failed as a lover, she had failed Dizz.

It wasn't till a month later that she found out she'd had lots of company at failing Dizz. After a half dozen abortive attempts she had wept and confessed her shame.

"Don't be foolish, Chris. You're better than anyone I've ever had," she'd said. "I just can't, darling. I never could."

Looking at it objectively, Chris knew she'd been a fool not to walk out then. But it was already too late. You couldn't call Dizz a habit. She was more like an addiction.

And when they'd gotten back to New York, Dizz had found them this gorgeous apartment. They'd settled into a pattern of something called living. Dizz, the beautiful wife, the perfect cook; the eternally bored dilettante, the artist, the music lover, the sculptor. Bored, bored, bored. And Chris. Solid, steady, plodding Chris. Hard-working and diligent, keeping her darling in cash enough to feed her whims.

But Chris had never been able to look at Dizz without little prickles of heat chasing up her spine. She could clench her fists and jam them in her pockets. But that didn't kill the tingling in her fingers, the yearning to reach out and grab Dizz and pull her close. Nothing could ease the pain of it.

It had been Dizz's idea that she go out that first Saturday night. She'd been blunt enough, Chris remembered. "Chris, if you want it —" Not that Dizz didn't care. She did. Oh, not about the sex part. Just that Chris was so vulgar about it. She got drunk first.

And that's how it had been for them. Dizz did

have her sentimental moments. She would creep into bed with Chris on Christmas Eve, sometimes even on a birthday. She would tease her with kisses. She would let Chris make love to her. But it never changed. The moment of greatest joy invariably became one of utter defeat.

Chris smiled wryly to herself. With all its frustrations, its denial, she knew she would not have missed a second of her years with Dizz. She was obsessed and she knew it. But she loved Dizz with all her being. She would always love her, even if George came back — even if Dizz left her.

There was a light rap at the door. It opened and Dizz stood there glowing. She had changed into a crisp blue dress that caught her essence and elaborated on it. She looked all soft and warm and ready to be loved. It was a long minute before Chris had the strength to sit up and get off the bed.

"Darling," Chris whispered. "You . . . you . . ." There were no words for what she was feeling. It stuck in her throat. It blinded her.

"Chris," the low voice vibrated. "I'm sorry I got upset about George. You know I didn't mean it." She moved very close to Chris, so close their thighs were touching and their breasts. "Darling, you do forgive me?"

Chris would have forgiven her a knife in the ribs. "Of course I do." She stood still, afraid to breathe, afraid Dizz would move suddenly and leave her alone.

"Darling," Dizz said, oh so tenderly. "Kiss me, darling."

I'm going mad, Chris thought. Stark, raving mad.

Chris put her arms around Dizz and gently held her tight. She kissed her and Dizz returned the kiss. They stayed close for a long time.

"Dinner's getting cold," Dizz murmured in her ear.

"Hmm. I guess it is." Chris murmured back. She could not let go of Dizz. She felt she might faint.

Dizz took her hand and led her out to the kitchen. Chris did not protest. She could put up with George, with anything — just so long as once in a while Dizz would look at her like that and touch her.

Nor did she question when Dizz got in bed beside her that night and snuggled close. They had spent a quiet evening of being pleased with each other. Too happy to think, Chris had let herself be mesmerized by the nearness, the very existence of Dizz.

She did not try to make love to Dizz. Being beside her in the dark, holding her close, pressing her lips to the baby soft hair was a more exquisite joy.

It was just before she fell asleep that Chris realized what was wrong. That it was only when she had found something new to interest her that Dizz knew contentment. And that the interest must be indeed profound to have produced an evening like this one.

Chris knew a moment of fear. She shivered in the suddenly cold room and pressed herself tight against the girl.

3

Chris finished her third cup of coffee and lit a cigarette. She had been sitting at the kitchen table for a half hour. She was fascinated. Dizz was cleaning out the oven, cleaning out drawers, cleaning out the sink. Dizz was cleaning and enjoying it.

"Chris, come get that platter down for me, will you?" Dizz paused to smile at her, then dampened the sponge in her hand and went back to the stove.

"Are we expecting company?" Chris said as she unwound from the chair and stood up. She walked to the cupboard and stretched to reach the platter. She set it on the table and returned to the chair.

"Not that I know of," Dizz answered. "I'm full of energy, that's all. You know I like to keep the house clean for you."

Chris picked the cigarette up from the ashtray and took a long drag. "What's the platter for?"

"Turkey. We haven't had it for ages. I thought you'd like it for a change." Dizz came over to the table and stood looking at her. She reached out a hand and ruffled the close-cropped hair on Chris' head. "Honey, in case it doesn't show, I like you sometimes."

Chris did not answer. It was too good to last, she knew, but why not enjoy it while she could?

The phone rang in the living room and Dizz moved to answer it. "I'll get it," she said.

Chris sat quietly smoking, not listening to the conversation. She knew without being told that the hiatus had ended. She wanted to drain it of every precious moment. She could not think beyond the second, beyond the reality of caressing Dizz and, for that second, possessing her.

Dizz came back into the kitchen and sat down facing Chris. She seemed suddenly subdued, yet her eyes betrayed an inner excitement. She folded her hands on the table.

"Darling," Dizz said, "that was George. He's driving up to Connecticut to see a client. He asked me to ride along."

"Are you?"

"Yes. He'll be here about noon."

That does it, Chris thought.

But she said nothing. She put out the cigarette.

Then she picked up the platter, stepped to the cupboard and returned it to the top shelf. She went through the living room and out to the terrace.

The garden, she thought. There's enough to be done to keep me busy all afternoon. Dig up those bulbs and get them inside. Should have some straw. Some fertilizer.

She turned back to the house. Dizz was standing at the door watching her.

"Chris, what's the matter?" Dizz said quietly. She stood aside to let Chris pass.

"Who said anything's the matter?" Chris was in no mood for this. But she knew Dizz would force the issue.

Chris crossed to the couch and sat down. Dizz sank into the sling across from her and leaned forward.

"I wish you'd hit me or something when you're feeling like this," Dizz said. "I can't stand it when you get sullen."

Chris sighed and leaned back. She shoved her hands deep in her pockets and stretched out her legs.

"Damn it, say something," Dizz said. "Talk to me."

"What would you like me to say, Dizz?" Chris replied.

Dizz sat back in the chair and glared at her. "Don't play games with me, Chris. Say it and get it over with."

"To be perfectly honest, I can't think of a thing."

"Darling," Dizz said, "do you really think that you have any reason to feel insecure?"

"No," Chris said slowly. She knew that Dizz had been faithful to her. She had no reason to doubt her now. But there was a terrible sickness in Chris. Something pounded in her head, an ugly something. What, it said, will happen to me if he can do for her what I can't? What if she goes to bed with him and finds out what it means to be fulfilled? It's not very likely to happen, I know that. But it could. It could!

"Then, darling," Dizz went on, oblivious to the voice in Chris' head, "Why are you so upset? All that's going to happen is that I'll have a nice drive in the country. Even you can't find anything ominous in that."

Wanna bet, Chris thought. But all she said was, "I guess I'm just being silly."

"Of course you are," Dizz said earnestly. She got up out of the chair and came to sit by Chris. She ran a long pointed nail around Chris' ear and down her neck over the bruise.

Chris took the finger in her own. "Don't distract me," she said.

Dizz turned on that smile and it hit Chris where it hurt. She leaned over and pecked Chris quickly on the lips. "So you won't be jealous, will you?" she said.

"Look, honey," Chris said. "You know all I care about is that you should be happy. If it makes you happy to go out with George, go. What more can I say?"

Chris had no more to say that she wanted Dizz to hear. She dared not tell her that she was afraid, and that it was not George who made her so, but her own sense of inadequacy. She could not tell Dizz, who had never known it, of the kind of thing that happened when two people fulfilled all each other's needs. She had prayed that Dizz would never know it with somebody else. She had hand-picked their friends to include no one who might tempt her away. But George was something she hadn't counted on. And Dizz was obviously attracted to him.

Dizz curled up beside Chris and put her head against Chris's shoulder. "Well, anyhow, we'll be home early. You don't mind eating out this once, do you?"

Chris moved her head to look down at Dizz. "No, darling," she said, "I don't mind." She felt herself slipping. Dizz was so soft, so sweet. She wanted Dizz to have fun and come home early. Maybe she'd even be glad to get home.

Chris slid her arm around Dizz's waist and Dizz nestled against her. Their heads were close together. We fit so well, Chris thought. We belong this way. And she felt that Dizz must know it too.

Dizz moved after a while and went to her room to dress. She had left the door open and for a few minutes Chris sat watching her. Then very deliberately she rose and went back onto the terrace.

A black and white cat from across the alley was perched on a corner of the fence taking the sun. Somebody's radio blared out an orange juice commercial. Brakes squealed somewhere out on the Avenue. It seemed like any other Monday morning.

Yet Chris knew in her heart that it wasn't. Dizz was too happy, too anxious. She found herself hoping that Dizz would be disappointed and come home miserable and take a couple of drinks. That Chris could cope with, but this other thing she could not touch.

She sat down on a garden chair and proceeded to ignore the whole situation. She looked at the cat. She

27

listened to street sounds and some terrible thing of Bach's. She smoked herself nauseous.

The buzzer rang in the kitchen. She bent her head to hear if Dizz would run, a little too eagerly, to answer it. But it was quiet in the apartment.

"Honey," Dizz called out the window. "Get it, will you? I'm not quite ready."

An hour and she's not quite ready. An hour. A person could try on everything in Macy's in that length of time.

Chris got to the kitchen just as the buzzer sounded the second time. She pushed the button and opened the door. George took off his hat as he came through the doorway. He stood with it hanging from two fingers and stuck out the others in greeting. The left hand was behind his back.

"Hi, Chris," he said with that ear-to-ear grin. "I brought a friend." He took his left hand from behind his back and held out the friend for inspection.

"It's adorable," Chris laughed and in half a second she was sitting on the living room floor getting acquainted. The miniature schnauzer couldn't have been more than two months old. He still looked a little wobbly. With his shiny eyes and little tufted self, he enchanted Chris completely.

"His name's Schnitzel," George said, squatting on the floor beside Chris. He held out a hand and the pup bounced over to it and licked his fingers. "He's just learning manners. Better not let him get too excited."

Chris sat back on her heels and watched the pup. "I don't imagine he can do too much damage," she said.

George picked up Schnitzel and got to his feet.

"I'm beginning to think he could win a medal," he said.

"Chris, are you quite comfortable?"

Chris heard the icicles in Dizz's voice and looked up rather foolishly from her seat on the floor.

George turned quickly. "Hello, Sheila," he said. He took a step forward, cupping Schnitzel in his hand. "Chris and my buddy have just been saying hello." Dizz turned on the charm. "Oh, he's a love," she cooed. She put out a hand and played with the puppy's ear. "Isn't he darling, Chris?" she said, turning to look down at her friend.

Chris stood up and nodded at Dizz. She had a smirk on her face that she knew Dizz could kill her for. "Yes, he is," she said. "And I'm so glad you like dogs. I gather you'll be holding the baby this afternoon."

George smiled happily at Dizz. "I'm glad you do too," he said. "I've had one or another all my life." He put out his hand and gave the pup to Dizz.

Dizz took the pup and cuddled it in her arm. She stroked it lovingly with the other hand.

Chris turned away to find a cigarette. She could not look at Dizz and keep a straight face. Dizz with a dog! It was too delicious. Dizz with one of those dirty smelly beasts that she could not tolerate.

"Chris," Dizz said, "would you get my coat for me, dear? The light blue one."

"Of course," Chris answered and went to the closet off the kitchen. She took the coat and put it over her arm. She walked back to Dizz.

Dizz took advantage of the moment to glare at Chris with fury. "Thank you," she said stiffly as Chris draped the coat over her arm.

29

"Well, I guess we're ready," George said. "I'm sorry you're busy this afternoon, Chris. Maybe you can make it next time."

Chris looked at Dizz. "I'm sorry too," she said.

Dizz did not look at Chris, but busied herself with Schnitzel. She flushed slightly, then said, "Goodbye, Chris. We'll be home early, I think. Won't we, George?"

"Should be," he answered. He turned to Chris. "Is it okay if I take the young lady to dinner on the way back?"

"Yes," Chris said. "It's okay."

"Then we'll see you later," he said. He took Dizz by the elbow and steered her to the door.

Chris closed the door behind them and stood with her back against it. She couldn't blame George, she knew. He was doing his best to play it fair. It was Dizz she should hate, if she wanted to hate somebody. But how the devil could she hate Dizz?

She walked into the living room and slumped onto the couch. She put out the cigarette. Her hands dug angrily into her pockets and she pushed her feet hard against the floor.

Whatever this game Dizz was playing, Chris did not like it. Chris did not mind a good fight with everything out in the open. But when a woman started being wily, a person might as well beat an honorable retreat from the battlefield.

Dizz had never done anything like this before. She was usually bluntly honest. Hurt like hell, sometimes. But at least you knew what was happening. You could only guess this way.

Chris didn't like any of the answers she came up with.

The phone startled her out of her bitter reverie. She leaned over to the end table and grabbed the receiver.

"Hello," she said.

"Miss Hamilton?" asked a voice she knew from somewhere.

"Yes."

"Chris, darling, this is Carol. I thought maybe you'd like to come help me with some sea shells over lunch."

Chris paused a long minute. She knew perfectly well she was too old to play at getting even. And she knew she had no business getting involved with this girl.

"Yes," she said. "I'd like that. Very much, in fact."

"Good," Carol said. "Can you be here in an hour?"

"Honey," Chris said, "I can make it in half the time, if you're free."

"Come ahead. I'll see you then."

Chris hung up the phone and hurried to put on a skirt. She knew it was all wrong. She belonged to Dizz and she always would. She could not decently let anyone else get interested.

Carol was a good kid. She deserved somebody who could love her, who would settle down with her.

Chris had all the arguments against it down pat. But she felt a niggle of excitement at the thought of being with Carol, of caressing her and loving her.

And when she closed the door behind her, she walked briskly to the corner to hail a cab, filled with a kind of elation she had not felt in years.

4

The meter made a dollar's worth of clicks before the cab left the crosstown traffic and turned north on Fifth Avenue. A dozen blocks later it pulled up in front of a four-story stone building that looked no different from the others lining the block.

A small metal placard on the great black door said MARINE MUSEUM.

"This the place?" asked the driver, turning to peer at Chris through smudgy thick lenses.

"Yes, this is it," she answered, leaning across to open the door.

"Don't look much like a museum," he commented sourly.

"It's private," Chris whispered confidentially and turned on a mysterious smile.

"Oh," the driver said. The awe in his voice made Chris at least an ambassador from lower Mongolia.

Chris grinned and handed him two singles. She stepped out of the cab and slammed the door without looking back.

She felt the driver watching her till she had climbed the wide concrete steps, opened the heavy black door and passed inside.

It was always an experience to enter this place. Something like being suddenly at the bottom of a tropic sea. The walls were tapestried in warm blues and greens with an occasional splash of scarlet and of gold. The floor was covered with a thick sand-colored carpet that caught and held every trace of noise. The great entry hall rose four stories high and from the skylights above long fingers of sunlight reached down, only occasionally finding bottom and resting there.

Beyond the hall and on the floors above was housed one of the finest collections of marine lore in the world. With almost limitless funds and a practical approach to spending them, Jonathan Brandt had put old Hobbes' will and his mansion to splendid use. In his employ divers had combed every sea, searching out lost cities, fabulous treasures and sea creatures of every variety. Thousands of books, maps, diaries and secret documents had found their way into his eager hands.

And the whole had been arranged in a fairy-tale fashion that never ceased to delight Chris and others who, for a rather sizeable fee, had the standing of lifetime members. It was like a casual visit to Neptune's private palace and being allowed to wander at will through his gardens and libraries. No showcases, no locked cabinets. The glories of the sea were all set within easy reach to be examined and admired.

Chris herself had been responsible for many fine contributions, mostly rare shells and a few oddities like the collection of treasure maps she had routed out in odd corners of the world. As she crossed the hall toward the office at the back, Chris was remembering proudly how she'd done that lying bastard Blackfield out of an authentic pirate's map. He'd tried to chisel her out of a small fortune. But he had a weakness for rum and poker. So . . .

"Chris!" A high-pitched squeal called to her. "Chris, dahling!" Jonathan Brandt had appeared, apparently from nowhere. He looked like a chubby cherub, all five-five of him round and pink and snub-nosed and somehow angelic. Little wisps of faded blonde hair poked out at the edges of his bald pate and his clear blue eyes would never get as old as the rest of him.

He bustled noiselessly across the carpet toward Chris, stretched forward on his toes and puckered his lips.

Chris bent to receive the greeting. She was fond of Jonathan, in a peculiar way. He was charming and pleasant and did his work expertly. But she wouldn't trust him out of her sight.

"Chris, it's been an age. You look marvelous, just too too marvelous," he said breathlessly. He always sounded breathless. "And how's Sheila?"

Chris felt a pang of dismay. Jonathan had known

Dizz for years, had even fancied himself in love with her once. He'd been one of the people who'd introduced them. She didn't like to think what might happen if he knew why she was at the museum.

"Sheila's fine," she said. "As always."

"Good, good," he said. "And what can we do for you this lovely afternoon? If anything." He stood with his hands together as if in prayer. He moved up on his toes, back on his heels. He was never still.

"Well," she paused imperceptibly, then took the plunge. "I got a call from your new assistant, Miss Martin. She's cataloging that last batch I brought in, I gather, and wants some information."

Dr. Brandt pursed his lips and clucked. "Very thorough, Miss Martin, very thorough. I've been most pleased with her work." He peered up at Chris. "Beautiful girl, beautiful. Have you met her yet?" he asked.

"No, I haven't," Chris lied. She prayed in her heart that Carol would play it smoothly when the time came for introductions.

"Come along, then. She's in the office in back." Jonathan turned toward the rear of the building.

Chris followed him the length of three immense rooms and through an archway into what had once been the solarium. There was not a sound to betray their passage.

When they entered the room, Carol was sitting on a high stool at a semi-circular counter that ran the length of the glass wall. Spread out before her on sheets of off-white paper were thousands of colorful pea-sized shells. She held one of these tiny shells between two fingers and was studying it intently.

Dr. Brandt coughed politely in order not to startle the girl.

Carol put the shell carefully on the paper and turned to face them. She looked up at Chris and began a smile that could easily turn out to be too friendly.

Chris sent her a warning with her eyes over Dr. Brandt's pink dome. Carol caught it. The smile eased to one of polite greeting.

"Miss Martin," Dr. Brandt said, then turned to Chris with a flourish of his hand, "this is Christopher Hamilton." The tone in which he said it implied that anybody but a fool would grasp the full significance of the moment.

Carol slid off the stool and came toward Chris as though she were about to curtsey to the Queen. "How do you do, Miss Hamilton," she said. Chris could see the laughter bubbling in her eyes.

Chris extended her hand. "Miss Martin," she said.

Solemnly they shook hands.

"Well, ladies," Dr. Brandt said, "I'll leave you to your work." He turned to go.

"Jonathan," Chris called after him, "one second. After I astound and bore this young lady to death with all the pertinent facts, have I your permission to buy her a drink?" She grinned at him. "I like to be on the good side of your assistants. I give them enough dirty work to do."

"Of course, Chris," he answered. Chris made a habit of Christmas gifts and the like, he knew. He turned importantly to Carol. "As soon as you've finished here, call it a day," he said expansively.

Chris watched him trot out through the archway and toward his own office off the foyer.

37

She turned to Carol. "Thank you," she said. "That fat little gentleman has all the instincts of a peeping Tom. And I can't see any good reason for keeping him posted on my personal life."

"Sure. Any time," Carol said. She walked back to the counter. "Does he know Dizz?" she asked, carefully keeping her eyes focused on the shells.

For a long minute Chris did not answer. She looked intently at the back of Carol's head, trying to calculate what was happening inside it. "Yes, he does," she said. "Why?"

"Just curious," Carol answered.

Chris came and stood beside Carol at the counter. She gripped the edge with both hands and pressed till the knuckles went white.

"Look," Chris said softly, "I came here because I wanted to see you. I like you," she said. "A lot. Do I have to give you the history of my life? Or will you take it for what it's worth?"

Carol tilted her head and smiled into Chris' eyes. "No, darling," she said. "I don't need any explanations. I just don't want you to get in trouble with your girl." She grinned impishly. "I know how unreasonable women can be."

Chris laughed and hastily planted a kiss on Carol's forehead.

"Now, big shot, we've got work to do." Carol turned to a rack of rolled maps, selected one and lifted it off. "Sit down over there at the desk and we'll get at it."

Chris reached out and easily lifted the cumbersome map from Carol's hands. She carried it to the desk and unrolled it on the broad top. Carol brought over a couple of conch shells to anchor the bottom corners.

"Now, I could use some tracing paper and a sharp pencil," Chris said. She stood looking down at the map, tracing with a forefinger the area to be lifted.

Carol came up behind her and laid a two-foot square of tracing paper over the map. Then she reached in front of Chris and pulled open the middle drawer. "Take your pick," she said.

Chris selected a blue drawing pencil and felt the lead with her finger. Then she took a contraption with a razor blade from the drawer, flicked lightly at the lead and tested it again.

"Okay," she said. "An ashtray and we're all set."

For two hours Chris bent studiously over the map, tracing carefully every minute particular of the Keys, shading here and there, labelling each area she had explored and listing meticulously which shells came from which spot. Occasionally she paused to take a drag on a cigarette or to sharpen the pencil.

Carol, she knew, was somewhere behind her, silently going about her business, not humming or running a sweeper or something, as Dizz would be doing.

Finally Chris straightened up and put the pencil down on the desk. "How's that?" she said.

Carol was all of a sudden at her elbow, studying the tracing. "Perfect, darling," she said. "You just saved me a week's work." She picked up the paper and carried it to the counter. She checked a couple of items against the key, shifted one to another sheet.

Chris rolled up the map, crossed with it to the rack and set it in place. She returned to the desk, moved the conchs back on a shelf, then sat down in the swivel chair.

Carol came and perched on the desk beside her. "It's a pleasure to watch you work, Chris," she said. "You're so thorough. And you know what you're doing."

"I should," Chris answered. "I've been doing it for twenty years."

"My God, I was just out of diapers then," Carol laughed. "What got you started?"

Chris shifted in the chair. "Well," she said, "a kind of childhood compassion, I guess. I was brought up around the Indian River Inlet, you know. Plenty of ocean and beach and dunes. I remember when I was just a little kid, going with my family to Long Neck to dig clams. Not in the mud on shore, but wading up to your neck in the water with a tub tied to you and floating behind. You dig down in the mud with the clam rake and when you're a kid it's fun to see if you can dig faster than the clams and catch 'em before they get away."

She paused to put out a cigarette. "Then one night I had a peculiar dream," she went on. "A big clam was standing in the water with a people rake and I was trying to dig my way down into the mud. And just when I thought I was safe, he grabbed me with the rake and pulled me out of the water and threw me in the tub." She laughed. "I never went clamming after that."

Carol slid off the desk and stood up. "But you started collecting clam shells?" she said.

"Hmm. And other kinds. And making maps. I used to walk along the shore, listening to the ocean. I'd hear voices, you know, telling me about far away

40

ports and all kinds of mysteries at the bottom of the sea." She sighed wistfully. "I even wrote poetry in the wet sand at one point."

Carol was silent, letting Chris enjoy her reverie.

"So," Chris said in a moment. "And now I'm hungry. How about you?"

Carol crossed to a small lavatory at one end of the office. "I'll be with you in two seconds," she said. And in two seconds she returned. She had put on a soft rose wool coat that set off her dark hair dramatically.

Chris lifted an eyebrow in approval. She was vaguely aware of a warmth of feeling toward this girl that she usually associated only with Dizz. It wasn't something that she could define. But it had something to do with wanting to protect her, to be strong yet infinitely tender.

Dizz had taught Chris to hide this feeling, to put it away or be laughed at. Yet Chris knew instinctively that Carol would not laugh.

"Chris, tell me something," Carol said as she came toward her. "And I'm not being catty."

"Okay," Chris said. "Ask away. I don't have to answer, after all."

"Does Dizz go with you on these trips? I mean, is she interested in your work?" Carol asked.

"Dizz?" Chris laughed deep in her throat. "Dizz doesn't know a conch from a cochina. And the only oyster she's ever see was on a plate in front of her. I thought she was a comrade when I met her, but I found out later she'd read up for the occasion." She said it affectionately, without malice. "But how come we're back to Dizz?"

"Frankly, darling, I'm just sizing up the

competition," Carol said. She put out her hand. "Let's go, handsome."

"After you, m'dear," Chris rejoined, bowing from the waist and waving her arm toward the arch. She stepped up beside Carol and took her elbow.

Together they walked out to the hall.

5

Chris let the heavy black door close quietly behind her, then hurried to follow Carol down the steps.

It was already late afternoon and Fifth Avenue was beginning to buzz with the homeward dash of thousands of office workers. A long string of buses, with taxis making links in the chain, honked and rattled down the Avenue. At the near corner a timid little woman peered desperately in both directions, looking for a break, then lifted an umbrella in one hand and her skirt in the other and launched into the fray. Miraculously she appeared on the opposite curb and lifted her nose contemptuously at the obscenities roared after her.

Carol stopped at the corner and faced Chris. "Darling," she said, "may I make a suggestion?"

"Of course."

"Let's go to the zoo. We can have lunch in the cafeteria."

Chris smiled at her approvingly. "Honey," she said, "that's perfect."

They walked to Sixty-fourth and crossed at the light. They went through the entrance, down the steps and turned right toward the monkey house. They walked slowly past the cages, not talking, pausing occasionally to chortle at the antics of the apes.

Carol had linked her arm through Chris' and when they stopped for a moment, she pressed close to her side. There was a good six-inch difference in height. Chris looked down at the girl now and then, feeling deeply contented and at peace. Something about Carol made Chris feel taller and stronger and for the moment sure of herself.

They passed the archway by the bear cages and went up the steps to the cafeteria. Only a few hearty souls sat at the tables on the terrace. The wind had come up and the fading rays of the sun gave little warmth.

"Outside or in?" Chris asked, stepping away from Carol to let a six-year-old with dog fly past.

"Outside, of course." Carol walked to a table for

two by the wall and plunked down her purse to claim possession. Chris followed and stood by the table as Carol took a seat.

"What shall I bring you?" Chris asked. She liked the way Carol let her take over.

"Let's see," Carol gave a thoughtful frown. "They have good chopped liver. And a piece of cake and a light coffee."

"Right."

Chris turned and passed through the large center doorway. Five minutes later she emerged carrying a heavy tray.

She set the tray on the next table and moved four sandwiches, two enormous slices of chocolate cake, four cups of coffee, napkins, sugar and silver on the table for two.

"You must be as expensive to feed as a Great Dane," Carol commented blandly.

"Worse," Chris grinned. She knew this was not true. Dizz always complained that she was a picky eater. She always was when Dizz was around.

Chris did not say another word until she was at the far end of three sandwiches, a piece of cake and two cups of coffee. Then she lit a cigarette, leaned back and said, "Ahh!"

Carol laughed delightedly. She sat looking across the table at Chris, an expression on her face that Chris had often yearned to see on Dizz.

In that moment Chris felt a sudden terrible fear. She knew what was happening to her and to Carol. Knew that she had never felt such contentment as at this moment. Even last night, holding Dizz, it had been edged with poignancy and pain. There was no pain now. Only joy. And it made her afraid.

She shivered and the cigarette fell from her fingers. She put out her foot and ground the butt into the floor.

"Darling," Carol said, "what on earth's the matter? You're green."

"I was thinking how much I enjoy being with you," Chris said.

"Is that something to have a fit over?" Carol asked her quietly.

"Yes, it is," Chris answered bluntly. She stood up shakily and held onto the table. "Come on. I'll take you home."

Carol made no comment, but followed Chris docilely down the steps, back past the cages and around to the entrance. At the bottom of the steps Chris paused and turned to face her. There was a gentle smile on Chris' lips and tender affection in her eyes.

"Carol darling, please forgive me," Chris said. She took both of Carol's hands in her own and pulled the girl close. "I don't always behave like an overgrown brat."

Carol nodded, "I know," she said. "Look, honey. I've got a couple of theories about what's eating you. They may be miles off base, but they'll do for the time being." She stepped away from Chris, but held onto one hand. "Right now, we could both use a drink. I've got a fresh bottle of bourbon at home." She wrinkled her forehead quizzically. "That is, if you have time."

"I have time," Chris said.

Hand in hand they took the steps by twos. Chris

flagged a cab and held the door for Carol, then stepped in behind her.

"Seventy Second and First," she said to the driver.

They rode in silence, each tucked in her own corner of the seat. Chris sat gnawing her lower lip and gazing intently out the window at nothing. For some inane reason she was thinking back to the party, the night she met Dizz. Trying to recapture that first emotion, to feel out the magic that had trapped and held her. She saw the lovely face, touched the soft hair, heard the vibrant voice whispering, saying . . .

"Chris, we're here," Carol said softly, touching her lightly on the arm.

Chris reached a hand toward her pocket.

"I already paid it," Carol said. She leaned across Chris and opened the door. "Come on, honey."

Chris got out and turned to help Carol. She shut the door and followed Carol toward the entrance of the old brick building.

The hallway smelled of onions and cats and garbage. Somewhere upstairs a woman was screaming at her husband. A kid was bawling. The steam press next door in the laundry hissed rhythmically. It was like all the crummy buildings in all the crummy neighborhoods Chris had known before Dizz happened. And for one nostalgic moment she relished the stench and the charm and the horror of it.

Carol stopped to peer into the mailbox for number ten. "Cobwebs," she said. "Once a month I get a phone bill."

Chris followed her up three flights of steps. She waited while Carol fished out the key from her purse, then reached to take it from her. She unlocked the door and pushed it inward, stepping aside to let Carol precede her.

Carol dropped her purse on top of the phonograph and crossed to a cabinet against the far wall.

"Come in and sit down," Carol said. She stooped to open the bottom compartment and lifted out a bottle. "Straight, on the rocks, mixed, what?"

"Straight," Chris answered. "And long." She walked to the sofa and sat down carefully on the edge. She crossed her hands on her knees.

Carol picked two glasses from the top of the cabinet and turned them over. With a bottle opener she broke the seal on the bottle. She carried the bottle and the two glasses over to the coffee table in front of Chris.

"Well, don't you look comfortable," Carol said. "I won't bite, you know." She looked down at Chris fondly. "Will you pour, madam?"

Chris leaned forward and wiggled the cork out of the bottle. She poured a third of a glass and handed it to Carol. Then she filled the other glass level full and bent to take a sip.

They sat side by side on the edge of the couch. Neither of them spoke or drank. Chris could hear a faucet dripping behind the screen that shut off the tiny kitchen. The woman was still screaming at her husband. The baby cried.

Carol laid a hand on Chris' arm and shook her gently. "Honey," she said, "would you like some coffee? I don't think you care for my bourbon." She pouted playfully.

"Coffee would be fine," Chris said. She put a finger under Carol's chin and tilted the girl's face to

48

look into her own. "And I do like your bourbon. But I'm trying to think about something and for once in my life I don't feel like being polluted."

"At least we're making progress," Carol said. She got up and walked behind the screen. "Instant okay?" she called.

"Naturally."

Chris sat listening to the clink of dishes, a spoon against a jar, the lid of a sugar bowl. Then water scalding into cups. The gurgle of milk from a bottle.

Carol carried the steaming cups to the low table and set them down. She took the bottle and glasses and put them back on the cabinet. Then she came and sat down beside Chris.

Chris had not moved from her stiff, uncomfortable position.

"Darling," Carol said, "may I have a cigarette?"

Chris took a pack out of her pocket, pulled out two and lit them both. She handed one to Carol. She crumpled the empty pack and dropped it on the table.

Then she turned to face Carol. "Carol," she began, "I think there are a few things we'd better settle."

"Before you say anything, Chris, let me put in my two cents' worth." Carol put her palms flat on Chris' clenched fists. "I'm sort of a shameless slob, darling. I love you and I admit it. But I know that you're in love with someone else. I think it's a sick kind of love or an obsession or something."

Chris attempted to move from under Carol's hands.

"No, Chris, listen to me," Carol said. "I think this because I've seen you blind drunk and miserable. Because I've got black and blue marks all over me where you let out your frustrations. Because, when you were sobering up and ashamed of what you'd done, you lay in my arms and sobbed like a baby." She paused to look at Chris closely. "How long has it been since Dizz let you make love to her?"

Chris looked away quickly. She did not answer.

"I thought so," Carol went on. "She doesn't satisfy you that way. She doesn't give a damn about your work. Yet you cling to her like she was —" She could find no words to describe it. "What difference does it make? That's your business. What I started to say is simply that I love you. I don't know if I can beat this thing that Dizz has become to you. I don't know if I can take you away from her. In fact, I won't even try. I hope you'll come to me because you want to be with me. Because I know, whether you'll believe it or not, that you will want to and, if you do, you'll be happy here."

"Are you finished?" Chris asked coldly.

"One more thing," Carol answered. "I know you can walk out of here tonight and never come back. But if you do, Chris, you'll be kidding yourself." She smiled at Chris. "Now, darling, what were you going to say?" She took both cigarettes and put them out in the ashtray.

Chris sighed tiredly. "I was going to say that when I leave here tonight, I will not be coming back. That I'm in love with Dizz and that I always will be. That I enjoy being with you. It's fun. But I'm only kidding myself because I know it won't get us anything but misery." She looked down at Carol and laughed. "I feel a little foolish."

Carol laughed too. "Now will you please kiss me? If there's anything I can't stand it's a lot of talk."

50

Chris went to the girl willingly. She put her arms around Carol and for a long minute held her tight. Then she kissed the girl deeply and long.

They lay together on the couch, Carol nestling in Chris' arms. Outside it had gotten dark and cold. Only an occasional bus rumbling down the street broke the stillness.

"Chris?"

"Hm?"

"It's getting late."

"Um, hmm."

"Dizz is waiting for you."

"Um, hmm."

"Chris?"

"Hm?"

"When will I see you again?"

Chris was silent for a moment. "That depends," she said. "We'll have Saturday night at least. Maybe sooner. I'll call you tomorrow."

"But you will be back?"

"Yes, Carol, I'll be back."

6

Chris stood by the fence at Beekman Place, gazing down to the river. She watched the red and blue of a Pepsi Cola sign ride the ripples from the far shore. Somewhere down near the island a boat hooted mournfully into the dark night.

She put her forehead against the wire and pressed her nose through the criss-cross hole. She put her fingers into other criss-cross holes and leaned heavily against the fence. She could barely stand.

She knew it had been a serious error of judgment to bolt that glass of bourbon just before she left

Carol. All the way home in the cab she'd clung to the door, her nose and forehead pressed to the icy window. Now she clung to the fence, as mournful as the foghorn, scared to walk in the house and face Dizz. She was drunk.

She felt in her jacket pockets for a cigarette, then remembered that she had emptied the pack.

A light mist had started a few minutes before and already her hair was damp and blowing into matted curls. Her feet were clammy and a chill ran through her body. It was past midnight. Still she did not move to enter the house.

She heard the click of heels on the sidewalk behind her. She did not turn to investigate them.

"I thought I might find you here," Dizz said softly. She came up close behind Chris and slipped an arm around the girl's waist. "Honey, come in the house. I've got some coffee going. You'll catch cold out here."

"Dizz, I'm drunk. I feel awful. I better stay here awhile." Chris spoke thickly, slurring the words.

"I know," Dizz said. "Come in the house. We'll sober you up." She spoke to Chris as though to a child.

Chris pulled away from Dizz and turned to lean against the fence. "Dizz," she mumbled, "do you hate me? Do you hate me because I'm a drunken slob?"

"Of course I don't hate you, you big fool." Dizz laughed softly. She moved close to Chris and put her head against the girl's shoulder. "Would I be snuggling up in front of the neighbors if I hated you?"

Chris thought that over carefully in her muddled, feverish brain. She knew that Dizz generally had a

53

motive when she snuggled up. But she was too far out to figure any angles at the moment. So she'd have to take Dizz's word for it.

Chris bent her head to press her lips to the girl's hair. It tickled her nose and she sneezed.

"Bless you," Dizz said. She took Chris' hand and pulled at her gently. "Come on, baby. The coffee'll boil over."

Chris let Dizz lead her back to the apartment. She stumbled down the hall and through the door and into the living room. She fell face down on the couch.

Dizz took Chris' damp shoes and set them in the kitchen near the stove. She went to the closet in her room and returned with a maroon wool blanket. She came to the couch and sat down beside Chris, letting the blanket fall to the floor.

Dizz slipped the skirt down over Chris' hips and legs, then struggled with the jacket. She tossed both onto the sling chair, stood up and tucked the blanket snugly around the still figure.

The she bent down and kissed an earlobe.

She quietly left the room. In a few minutes she returned with a mug of steaming coffee and a tumbler containing her favorite home remedy. She put both down on the floor by the couch.

"Honey," she said, shaking Chris by the shoulder. "Honey, look at me."

Chris made a grunt that meant no.

"Chris, look at me. You're not going to die." Dizz knelt beside Chris and reached out a hand to smooth the rumpled black hair. "Please, baby."

Chris laboriously maneuvered her head around and

managed to open one eye. She stared bleakly at Dizz, closed the eye, and slowly opened it again.

"Good girl," Dizz said. "Now pick up your head. I want you to drink this." She held the glass before the open eye.

Between them they got Chris propped on one elbow and the tonic safely inside.

"Okay," Dizz said. "Fifteen minutes and you'll be fine."

In about twelve Chris made a beeline for the john. She had a pretty good remedy of her own.

She crept back into the living room and grinned sheepishly at Dizz.

Dizz burst out laughing and came to help Chris back to the couch. "May I join you?" she asked.

"Be my guest."

Dizz stepped out of her dress and threw it on top of Chris' things in the chair. Then she got under the cover with Chris and nestled into her arms.

It occurred to Chris that a couple of hours before Carol had been in the same position. But with Carol she had buried her face in the girl's neck and run her fingers lovingly over the warm breasts. With Dizz she would not dare. With Dizz she must find conversation.

"How's Schnitzel?" That was fair venture.

"He's just fine. Do you know, I actually got to like the little devil. And he was awfully good in the car. I thought he might get sick or something."

"And George?"

"He's just fine, too," Dizz said. "We stopped on the way back for dinner. There was an orchestra there and we danced a little. I wish you liked to dance, darling." She leaned her head against Chris' jaw.

"I used to," Chris said. "You told me once I looked like a clown."

"Oh, silly," Dizz laughed. "You know better than to listen to me when I'm annoyed."

"Sure," Chris answered. She did not admit that she no longer knew when that was. That, in fact, Dizz seemed annoyed with her or herself or just the whole damned world most of the time.

"Anyhow, we danced and ate and had a couple of drinks. I like George," Dizz said. "He's good company. Witty, intelligent. He seems to know something about everything." She paused, then went on enthusiastically. "Not just something, but enough to hold his own with experts." Her voice dropped to an impressive tone. "He was Phi Beta Kappa at Harvard, you know."

"What else does he do?" Chris asked with disarming innocence.

Dizz hesitated for just a second. "I'll ignore that remark," she said.

Dizz, Chris appreciated, was in rare good humor. It would not be safe to test it too far. But the bourbon or something had given her a sneaky courage. She decided to push on.

"Well," she said, "I thought maybe he does card tricks or parlor magic or some such thing that might bring him down to my level of comprehension."

Dizz turned to look at her, a puzzled frown on her beautiful face.

Chris remained serenely calm.

"Darling," Dizz said quietly, "have I made a *faux*

56

pas? Should I go stand in the corner or something?" She was trying hard to be flip, but there was a slight tremor in the lower lip.

Chris saw it and was immediately consumed by guilt. What a lumbering ass she was, to take Dizz when she was happy about something and make her wretched. Sometimes months went by before Dizz got excited about anything.

"Honey," she said smilingly, "you know better than to listen to anything I say when I'm annoyed."

"Annoyed about what?"

"Myself, for getting drunk. You go off and leave me for an afternoon and I behave like a child. Do all kinds of stupid things." At the moment she almost believed what she heard herself saying.

"But what on earth have you done?" Dizz asked, a little worriedly.

For ten seconds Chris tottered on the brink of confession. Then she said, "What doesn't matter. Just that I'm feeling especially proud of myself."

Dizz breathed a sigh of relief. "Well," she said, "It probably wasn't anything you haven't done before."

Chris looked at her closely, searching for the hidden barb behind the words. It was not often that Dizz spoke of her activities without condemning them. But she could find no malice on the gorgeous face.

Chris relaxed and laughed. "Sometimes you scare me, miss," she said. She pulled Dizz closer and hugged her affectionately. "And, honey, I didn't mean to pick on you. Or on George."

"I know, darling. And I didn't mean to babble on like that." She kissed Chris lightly on the cheek. "But let's forget about George."

"Gladly," Chris said. "How about a hot cup of coffee? I could use it."

Dizz crawled out from under the blanket and stooped to pick up the cup. "Would you like something to eat, darling? I've got some chicken and an apple pie in the refrigerator."

Chris put a hand to her aching head. "Oh, baby, don't mention food to me. I'll probably never eat again."

"That I doubt," Dizz said from the kitchen. She came back a few minutes later with two full cups and handed one to Chris.

Chris downed the strong black coffee in three gulps. "Thanks," she said.

Dizz handed her the second cup. "Dessert," she smiled.

Chris took a sip from the second cup of coffee. Her head was beginning to calm down. A few more minutes and she'd be feeling alive again.

Dizz moved Chris' clothes off the chair and carried them into Chris' room. She took her dress into her closet and hung it on a hanger behind the door. She was humming happily to herself and the smile on her face was from her heart.

Chris lay on the couch, watching her and pleased that her woman, for whatever reason, was in a light mood. At moments like this, rare as they were, she knew she was the luckiest person in the world to possess this woman.

Dizz came back into the living room. "I don't mean to be a spoil sport, honey," Dizz said. "But have you finished that article I was supposed to remind you about?"

Chris stared at her blankly for a moment, then

sat bolt upright. "My God, I forgot all about it," she said. "You were supposed to remind me a week ago."

"I forgot," Dizz admitted.

They both laughed.

Chris stood up unsteadily and started toward her bedroom. "Look, kid, I've got all the material I need. Would you mind using a little of that rusty shorthand you're always bragging about?" She looked at Dizz pleadingly. "I promised to deliver the blamed thing tomorrow." She leaned wearily against the door jamb. "And, frankly, I couldn't hit a typewriter key tonight if my life depended on it."

"You mean this morning, but I get the idea," Dizz said. "Hurry up, darling. I'll get some paper."

Chris returned with a sheaf of neatly hand-written notes. She sat down on the couch.

Dizz took a seat on the floor beside Chris and leaned a notebook on her crossed knees. She looked up at Chris, waiting for her to start.

Chris took a sip of coffee, then relaxed against the couch. She began to dictate.

It was almost six when Dizz pulled the last sheet from the typewriter. Chris was stretched out on the couch, sleeping soundly. She had lasted till about five, then collapsed apologetically.

Dizz stacked the sheets neatly on the end table. She moved to the couch and smiled down at the sleeping figure.

Chris grumbled and opened her eyes when Dizz tried to lie down beside her. Then she smiled like a contented baby and opened her arms wide.

Dizz crawled in beside Chris and moved tight against her. "All finished, baby," she whispered.

"Thank you, darling," Chris whispered back. Even

in her sleepy state, she felt the marvelous magic of Dizz begin to take possession of her. She buried her nose in the soft blonde hair and pressed her lips to the scalp.

Dizz stirred in her arms. She raised her mouth to Chris.

Chris held the girl close and brought her mouth down hard on the waiting lips. Their tongues met, searched. Like a whirlwind, desire grew in Chris. Her woman, lying in her arms, wanting her, wanting her, not turning away in disgust. Not stopping her eager hands.

Chris' elation knew no bounds. She had not touched Dizz like this, loved her like this, for many lonely, bitter months. She felt again the wild flow of passion she had felt that first night. Her body ached with the need to possess Dizz, to seek again the fulfillment they had never known together.

She put her lips against the soft smooth cheek.

"Dizz, darling, please," she whispered hoarsely.

"Yes, darling, yes. Love me, Chris. Love me."

For a long, long moment they were absorbed, lost in each other, oblivious of time, of the world, oblivious of everything but the moment. Then the aftermath, like the quiet after the storm. The predictable end. Dizz in the exquisite agony of frustration. Dizz staring into the darkness. And Chris alone and shivering in an exquisite agony of her own.

Lying behind Dizz, Chris put her arms around the girl's waist and bowed her head between the shoulders. Death would have been welcome at that moment.

Chris dug her teeth into her trembling lip and closed her eyes tight to hold back the tears.

7

The phone rang that morning at ten.

Dizz stirred, but did not wake up.

The phone rang again and again. Finally Dizz moved an arm and pushed back the covers. She sat up and groaned. Then she reached for the phone.

Through a cottony haze Chris heard Dizz speaking to someone. She gathered the call was for her.

"Is it important, Jonathan? She's still asleep." A long pause. "All right. Hold on a minute."

Chris felt Dizz sit down on the couch beside her

and tickle her ear with a fingertip. Chris swatted as though to brush away a fly.

"Chris, wake up," Dizz said sternly. "Jonathan's on the phone. I really can't figure out what he's trying to say. But he said to tell you Max is in town with something big."

"Max," Chris shouted. "Why didn't you say so?" She threw back the blanket and sat up. "Hand me the phone."

Dizz obediently did as she was told. Then she sat down on the couch, too curious not to listen.

Chris took the phone and barked into it, her voice thick with alcohol and not enough sleep. "Jonathan?" she said. "What's happening?"

"Chris, Max reached port this morning. He just called. He wants to see you. He wouldn't say much on the phone, of course." Dr. Brandt's voice rose to a shriek. "But he wants five thousand."

Chris whistled through her teeth. "What's he got? Neptune's triton?" For five thousand, Chris thought, that's the least we should expect.

"Humpf," sniffed Dr. Brandt. "I wouldn't give him five thousand if he'd found Atlantis. I told him we couldn't go over five hundred. He'll take it," he said smugly.

"Okay," Chris said. "I'll see him this afternoon. Same place?"

"Yes."

"Right. I'll get in touch with you later." Chris banged down the receiver and stood up. She started toward the bathroom. "Just coffee, Dizz. I'm in a hurry."

Dizz sat looking after her in amazement. "So I

see," she commented. "But you're not leaving here with a hangover and an empty stomach."

"Who's got a hangover?" Chris said from the bathroom. "I feel wonderful."

"Well, I've got one if you haven't," Dizz answered, following her into the room. She put down the lid on the toilet and sat down.

Chris turned on the hot water in the tub and flipped the handle on the stopper to "Closed." Then she turned to the sink, took a pink toothbrush from the cup holder and squeezed out a long strip of toothpaste. She brushed vigorously and rinsed her mouth.

"Well?" Dizz said.

Chris turned off the water and stuck an inquiring toe into the tub. She added a dash of cold. Without pausing to answer Dizz, she climbed in and began to work up a lather.

"Well?" Dizz said again.

"Well what?" Chris said.

"Don't be difficult. Who is Max?"

"Max is a man," Chris said.

Dizz clucked irritably. "Look, child, you never got this excited over a man in your life. Who is Max?"

Chris laughed. "Wash my back, will you?"

Dizz came and leaned over the tub. She took the wash cloth and the soap and gave the broad back a good scrub. Then she stood up.

"Well?" she said.

"Well what?" Chris answered.

"Oh, go to hell!" Dizz said and stalked out, slamming the door behind her.

Chris grinned and fished for the soap. She

lathered the cloth and briskly scrubbed one long leg, then the other.

She got a secret pleasure out of deviling Dizz that way. She knew it was mostly a sadistic urge, a desire to get even. For last night and for all the other nights, she had to hit back.

Chris frowned. Even in her frustration she knew it was not right to blame Dizz. God knows, Dizz isn't happy about it, Chris thought. The way she lies there, in an agony too thick for me to penetrate. A million miles away from me and from anyone who would try to help her.

Well, she sighed, not much I can do about that. Except live with it. And love her and want her and never really have her.

Chris opened the drain and stepped out of the tub. She picked up a towel and began to dry. She had put away her problem with Dizz and turned her thoughts to Max.

I hope it's something big, she thought. Something that'll get me away from a typewriter for a while and back into the sea.

By the time she had dried herself and combed her hair, Chris was full of hope. Hope for a chance to get away for a while, from Dizz and from George and from Carol and from herself, and back to the stillness and peace of the underwater world.

When Chris reached the kitchen, dressed and ready to go, Dizz had just finished scrambling eggs with bacon. She carried two plates from the stove to the table. "Sit down," she said.

Chris sat. "What's eating you?" she grinned.

"You make me so damned mad sometimes. What's

so mysterious about a bunch of stinking sea shells?" Dizz was furious and fuming.

"Who said anything about sea shells?" Chris picked up a fork and went at the eggs hungrily.

"Shut up. Just shut up!"

Chris finished her eggs and bacon and opened a fresh pack of cigarettes. She took one out and lit it. "Now, slavey, if you'll bring me some coffee," she paused and winked at Dizz, "I'll tell you about Max."

Dizz put a cup of coffee in front of Chris and set the pot in the center of the table. "So tell me," she said.

"Well," Chris said, reaching for the sugar, "his name is Max Peterson. Fifteen years ago he was the world's leading marine biologist. Now he's sort of a sea-going hobo." She paused to take a sip of the coffee.

"What happened?"

"He got married," Chris went on. "Six months later his wife had a miscarriage and died. It nearly finished him. He hit the skids, started drinking. For a couple of years he just sort of leeched off his friends, people he'd worked with. Then he went on the bum. For the past ten years he's been drifting around on freighters."

Dizz looked at her blankly. "And what makes this sot such a fascination to you and Jonathan?" she asked.

"He's not just a sot, Dizz. He's a genius in his field — marine biology, that is. And his special charm is that he's been responsible for some of the best finds we've made. Remember that black pearl I went after a couple of years ago?"

"Of course," Dizz said. "It's the most beautiful thing I've ever seen."

"He told us where to find it. He used to belong to the museum. Now he just comes around for money." Chris paused thoughtfully. "Though sometimes I think he still cares. Anyhow, he hasn't done any diving since he took up alcohol. He lost his nerve."

"And you think he's found another pearl?"

"He's found something, at any rate," Chris said.

Dizz got up and carried the dishes to the sink. She carefully avoided looking at Chris.

"Darling, does that mean," Dizz said slowly, "that you'll be going diving again?"

"It could," Chris said. "In fact, I hope so. I don't get much of a charge out of picking up shells on the beach anymore." She pushed back her chair and stood up. "Why?"

"Ever since that barracuda tried to make lunch of your leg, I've preferred to think of you diving in a quiet indoor pool," Dizz said.

Chris did not answer immediately. She was thinking of the scar on her leg and of the year she'd spent hobbling around the house. She had not forgotten the incident for one day of her life since it happened. It had nearly ended her career. And her.

Chris knew in her heart that she was as anxious as Dizz. But for a different reason. She had to find out, sooner or later, whether or not she was done for as a diver. This could be her chance.

"Dizz," Chris said, "look at me." She put her hands on the girl's shoulders and turned her around. She gazed down at her seriously. "Once you upset a pan of hot grease. You burned both hands and both thighs, and pretty badly too. Did you stop cooking?"

Dizz was silent for a long time. Then she said, "Okay, teacher. I understand the lesson for today." She looked up and smiled. "Just don't come home to me mauled."

"That's better," Chris said. "Now, I've got to get out of here."

Chris walked into the living room and picked up the typed manuscript. "I'll probably be gone all day," she said. "I have to deliver this, see Max, and then stop at the museum."

"Call me and I'll have dinner ready when you get here."

"Right." Chris gave Dizz a quick peck on the nose and started for the door. "See you later."

She left the house and turned right on Fiftieth, then right again on First Avenue. She walked rapidly, her hands deep in her jacket pockets, the manuscript under her arm. She had not worn a coat nor did she carry a purse. Her heels were flat. She was in a hurry and stripped for action.

At Fifty-Sixth she made a quick stop at the bank. When she came out, she was carrying five hundred dollars in twenty-dollar bills. She folded them in a neat wad and jammed it into her inside pocket.

Then she hailed a cab.

"Forty-Sixth and Lex,"she said. "Fast."

Two hours later she emerged from the offices of *Marine Life* irritated and beginning to suffer the first pangs of a hangover. She'd been kept waiting while Mr. Peale read, waiting while Mr. Peale conferred with Miss Macintosh, waiting while Miss Macintosh talked to Mr. Blutt, waiting while Mr. Blutt wrote out a check and gave it to Miss Macintosh who gave it to Mr. Peale who gave it to Chris. Then she had to wait for the elevator.

She went into a drugstore on the corner.

"Bromo," she said to the counterman.

"Bromo it is."

She swallowed the bubbles quickly, dropped a dime on the counter and went back out to the street.

She decided against a cab. Her head was in no condition. She turned west on Forty-Sixth and walked slowly toward Fifth Avenue.

People hurried all around her, bent on lunch hour shopping and business. A fat greasy woman in a yellow coat collided with her and swore at Chris over her shoulder. Chris sighed and walked a little faster.

A bus. She'd take a bus to Washington Square. The ride down Fifth was the only one in the city she could tolerate on a bus. Maybe if she closed her eyes . . .

She took a seat at the rear of the bus, next to the window. She rested her elbow on the window ledge and her head in her hand. The man behind her was reading the *Times,* folded lengthwise like you fold it hanging onto a strap in the subway. Every time the bus stopped, the edge of the paper hit her just below the neck. Stop, bump. Stop, bump.

She counted thirty-eight bumps before the bus rolled around Washington Square circle and stopped. The thirty-ninth came on schedule.

Chris walked to the ladies' room in the park. She got some paper from one of the booths, wet it at the sink, and pressed it against her eyes and her forehead. By now her head was not splitting — it had split. She took a small bottle of aspirin out of her pocket and shook out four. Then she scooped them into her mouth. She cupped her hands under the cold water, took a long drink and swallowed.

West on Fourth, south on MacDougal, west on Third, south on Sixth Avenue. Slow, walk slow, walk slow.

At the junction of Sixth, Bleeker and Carmine she went into a luncheonette and sat on a stool at the counter.

"Bromo," she said.

"Bromo it is."

She was beginning to feel about half human. It wouldn't pay to be shaky around Max. That boy was a shrewdie. He was out for money and plenty of it. You had to be with it to get what you came for.

She followed up the bromo with a cup of thick black coffee. She took her time. She raised a hand and looked at it. It was steady. When the rest of her felt the same way, she stood up.

She paid the man and went to the phone booth at the back of the shop. She dropped a dime in the slot and dialed Max's number.

After the tenth ring a voice croaked, "Yeah?"

"Max? This is Chris Hamilton."

"Where are you?"

"Downstairs."

"You got money?"

"Yes, I've got money."

"C'mon up."

Chris hung up the phone and left the store. She walked faster now, the headache for the moment forgotten.

8

Chris turned left on Bedford and into the entrance of an apartment house next to an Italian grocery. White X's on some of the windows marked the building condemned. In the store the fat grocer was exclaiming loudly in broken English about how he'd been here thirty years. His fat wife singsonged in mawkish chorus.

Inside was the smell of thirty years of garlic and more years of cabbage and grease and no garbage cans. The floor was grey with filth and smudged where someone had tracked a dog turd down the hall and up the stairs. Somebody else or maybe the same somebody had puked here long ago. The yellowish mess had dried to a crust on the wall and floor. A little boy stood among the ruins in grave dignity, relieving himself against the wall.

Chris swallowed hard. Every year it got worse. The first time she'd come here it was like being dropped into a garbage dump in July. That was eight years ago. There were no words anymore.

She climbed to the fifth floor and stopped at apartment twenty-one. Of all the dirty doors in the building, this was the dirtiest. She knew neither it nor the rooms inside had been cleaned in the eight years Max had had the place.

She bumped the door a couple of times with her foot. The door opened almost immediately.

Max Peterson was in his early fifties, a six-foot, pot-bellied, hairy, ape-like man. He had been handsome once, but now the tiny veins beneath his cheeks and around his eyes had broken and he looked like a sick purple chimpanzee. At the moment he was wearing a pair of filthy black trousers with a broken zipper, an undershirt and a thick stubble of beard.

Max swung open the door and bowed from the waist. "Chris, good to see you."

Chris took two steps into the room and stopped. Behind Max on the cot was a fat blonde in a brassiere. She was clutching the neck of a gin bottle in one hand. She was about twenty and had gorgeous green eyes.

The blonde looked straight back at Chris. She lifted the bottle and took a long drink. She wiped her mouth on the back of her hand.

"Excuse me," Chris said.

Max whirled to face the blonde. "For Pete's sake, Jennie, get some clothes on," he said savagely.

Jennie belched out a coarse sound. "What the hell for? That big dyke." She laughed nastily. "She's seen plenty o' this before."

"She didn't come here to look at you," Max said. "We got business to discuss."

Jennie got off the couch and came toward Chris, swinging the gin bottle. "How about it, handsome? I bet you'd rather talk business with me, huh?"

The smell of gin and sex and perspiration hung over the girl like a cloud. It moved with her as she sidled across the room. It surrounded the two of them as she came up to Chris and rubbed against her.

Chris flushed deeply. She had been approached by women like Jennie before, but never quite like this. Never with a straight man for an audience. Certainly not when the guy was the woman's lover and no doubt paying for her services.

But she knew she had to be calm about it, not take the damn slut and bat her around like she deserved. She had to be polite about it.

Chris put three fingers on each of Jennie's shoulders and pushed her gently away. "No, thanks," she said.

"Big, dumb bastard," Jennie said. "Big dumb bastard."

Max slammed the door behind Chris. He approached Jennie. His arm went up and back. The huge hand caught Jennie on the side of the head. She screamed and dropped the bottle. It smashed and gin soaked into the bare wooden floor.

Jennie glared at Max with hatred. "Big dumb bastard," she said.

Max grabbed her by the shoulders and propelled her toward a door at the other end of the apartment.

"Now get out of here," he said.

Jennie went into the other room and slammed the door. "Big dumb bastards," she yelled.

Max pushed the broken bottle under the sink with his foot. It brushed against a paper bag. A plump cockroach emerged and scuttled away across the floor.

"I'm sorry about that, Chris," Max said. "She's not very bright."

"Or very sober," Chris added. "Forget it."

Max pushed some rags that were probably clothes off a chair to the floor. He turned to Chris. "Sit down."

"Thanks," she said. She sat down without looking at the chair. It was easier that way. "Jonathan tells me you've got something that might interest us."

Max snorted. "What do you mean, might?"

Max pulled out a second chair and sat down by the table. He pulled a bottle toward him. "Drink?" he said.

"No, thanks," Chris said. "I'm on the wagon as of this morning's hangover."

"Wish I could say the same," he sighed. "It gets you after awhile." He poured some of the syrupy liquid into a glass with something on the bottom that looked like black coffee. He took a long drink.

Chris waited for a minute, then said, "So what have you got?"

Max leaned his chin on one hand and looked her straight in the eyes. "Ever seen a Glory-of-the-Seas?" he asked.

"Once, in a museum," she said. "There are only a couple of dozen of them around."

"Supposing I told you where you can find hundreds, maybe more?" Max said.

Chris felt an irresistible surge of curiosity. "Well," she said cautiously, "I might tell you you're drunk. Nobody's seen one alive since 1838. Or do you mean you've found the graveyard where all good little Glories went to die?"

"Alive, my dear, alive."

"Hundreds or more?" Chris said. "Alive? Let's hear it, Max."

Max leaned back against the chair. "Got a cigarette?"

Chris handed him one and held out a match. She left the pack on the table.

"Did you ever hear of a place called Tongariva?" he asked.

"Vaguely," she answered. "I could probably find it on a map."

He took a deep drag on the cigarette. "It's a small island in the south Pacific. It makes a triangle like this." He traced a triangle in the dust on the table top. "Here's Pago Pago, here's Tahiti," he pointed. "And up here at the top is Tongariva."

"I get the picture," Chris said. "So what? You know as well as I do that shell's only been found around the Philippines."

"That's ancient history," Max said.

"I'm listening."

"So I'm telling you," he said. "I was working on a freighter out of Valparaiso. This is about six months back. We hit a storm — it was March tenth, in fact. Well, anyhow, we got blown off course and the damned boiler blew up. We had to pull into Tongariva to make repairs."

He stopped to fill the glass again. "Still interested?"

"Go on, Max," Chris said.

"Well, the island itself didn't amount to much. But we had some of the natives helping us on the ship for a couple of days. One of them had this shell on a cord around his neck. Like a hunk of jewelry. I thought it was a Glory, but I couldn't believe it till I got him to take it off and let me have a look at it."

Chris picked up the pack of matches and began turning it over slowly in her fingers. She was no longer looking at Max. In the back of her mind she was already calculating how best to present this to Jonathan.

"Sure as hell," Max said, "there it was. You should have seen it, Chris." His eyes mellowed. "A big one, at least five inches. A pink pearly lip, perfect, smooth. And deep brown flecks and tan, with a rich warm gold." He was silent for a minute. "I've seen three in my time," he went on, "but this was the most beautiful."

"You're sure, Max?" Chris said.

"Damn it, of course I'm sure. I knew this business before you were born, kid," he said angrily, "and don't you forget it."

"Okay, okay. Take it easy."

He took another drink.

Chris stirred restlessly in her chair and shifted her feet. She wanted him to go on.

Max burped and then continued. "I could make a little talk-talk with the natives. This one had picked up some pidgin English at Tahiti, so between us we managed. He told me that in a kind of lagoon off the

76

southwest of the island were lots of these beautiful creatures. He said, 'Hull lot, like stars in sky!' "

"You just saw the one?" Chris asked.

"Yeah, sure. But this guy had nothing to gain by lying to me, after all," Max said. "He's not up on the par value of shells."

That sounded reasonable. "Go on," Chris said.

"There's not much more," he said. "Except that I went for a look at this lagoon. It's there, all right. I cruised the shore. Kicked up sand and looked under rocks. I didn't find any of the shells."

"But you didn't do any diving?" Chris said. She took a cigarette from the pack and lit it. She saw that her fingers were trembling and she knew she was more excited than she wanted Max to realize.

"No."

"So, in other words, if I go chasing off to Tongariva, it's possible that the only Glory I'll see is hanging around a native's neck on a cord."

"You don't believe that, Chris. Any more than I do," Max said. He wiped his nose on the back of his arm. "It's not very likely this native picked up the only Glory in the whole damned Pacific."

"I'm the cautious type."

"Look, according to this native, he found these things in the lagoon when he was out diving for oysters. He picked one up because it was pretty." He spread his hands. "They like trinkets and beads and stuff. You know. And if the animals were fit to eat, every native on the island would have a string of those shells around his neck. But they use other things, mostly cones, from snails they can eat. I don't have to tell you they don't have museums out there."

77

Chris smiled. She was inclined to agree with Max, as usual. He'd never been wrong yet. "Okay," she said, "I'll buy that. What can you tell me about the lagoon?"

Max nodded. "I checked on that. As far as I could find out, it's pretty good for diving. A lot of coral and rock, but you're used to that. It's cut off from the open sea by a reef, so there's not much chance you'll run into anything dangerous."

Chris dropped the cigarette onto the floor and ground it out with her toe. There wasn't any ashtray in the place.

"It sounds okay," she said.

She stood up. She reached into her inside pocket and took out the wad of bills. She dropped it on the table.

"Five hundred," she said.

"You ought to be able to do better than that," Max said.

She shook her head. "Nothing doing," she said. "Brandt told you what we'd pay."

Chris heard the door open at the other end of the room and looked toward it. Jennie came out and stood, leaning against the jamb. She had added a pair of black lace panties to her costume.

Max folded his hand over the wad of bills and moved it to his pants' pocket. "Get the hell outta here," he said to the girl.

"Oh, shut up. Who needs you?" Jennie said. She was sober now, and nasty. She kept looking at Chris, her eyes slowly and appreciatively sizing her up. She closed one eye in an elaborate wink. She stood waiting for a reaction.

Chris wanted to turn and run away from the

stench of Jennie, away from this filthy apartment and this degraded man.

Chris turned to look at Max. "Thanks," she said. "See you in about a year, I guess."

"Yeah," Max said. He got up from the chair and started toward the door.

"Leavin' so soon, big boy?" Jennie said to Chris. "Wait a minute and I'll go with you."

Chris felt her ears go hot. She knew they would be blazing red. She did not turn around.

Max stood facing the two of them, a malicious smirk in his bleary eyes. He watched Jennie undulate across the room to stand behind Chris.

Chris went rigid as Jennie's arms crept around her from behind. She felt the forehead against her back, the breasts, the thighs. Jennie's hands started at Chris' shoulders and began to trace down the outline of her body.

"I can show you a good time, big boy," the girl said in a throaty whisper.

Chris felt the cloud of gin and stench surrounding her. She gagged with revulsion deep inside herself. She reached up and grabbed the girl by the wrists and leaned forward sharply to propel the body away from her.

"Bastard," Jennie snarled.

Chris walked to the door, then stopped and turned to look at the girl. She grinned broadly. "Big dumb bastard," she said.

Max opened the door. "So long, Chris," he said.

"Right," Chris said. She went out through the doorway and heard a slam behind her. Then a slap. Then a scream.

Chris smiled to herself and shook her head sadly.

It pained her to think that a guy like Max could get so fouled up on whiskey and women.

But she couldn't be bothered with philosophy. She had work to do. Jonathan was waiting to hear from her. And he'd take a lot of convincing.

9

By the time she reached the street, Chris had already figured out most of the twenty questions Jonathan would ask her. And for most of them she had answers. But there were a couple of details she knew she'd better check on.

For all she knew Max might have invented the whole thing. He might never have seen Tongariva except on a map. She had nothing to go on except the story he'd told her. And Jonathan, before he doled out the museum's cash for an expedition, would want more than that.

Not that she didn't trust Max. She did, or at least she almost did. Max had an uncanny way of hitting on things like the black pearl and the Glory-of-the-Seas, born out of a combination of curiosity and greed. As long as the curiosity remained the stronger, Chris could depend on Max and expect to find whatever he sent her after. But for years now she'd been waiting for him to slip, to invent something plausibly fantastic for the sake of a fast buck.

At the corner Chris picked up a late edition and dropped a nickel on the pile of papers. She walked rapidly back to the luncheonette and went inside. She took a seat at the counter.

"Coffee," she said.

"Reg'lar?"

"Yes."

She leafed through the paper from the back, then down the list. Only one South American freighter had made port this morning. The *Bolivar*. Now all she had to do was find a sailor who had been on board.

Chris swallowed the coffee in three gulps and went back out to the street. She tossed the paper into a trash basket and hailed a cab.

Ten minutes later the cab stopped on South Street, in front of the Seamen's Home. Chris got out and hurried under the figurehead of Sir Galahad and inside. Emery Tuttle was at the desk. He had helped her often before; had found her an assistant for the Tortugas deal.

"Good afternoon, Miss Hamilton," Emery said.

"Hello, Emery," Chris answered. She put her

elbows on the desk and leaned across, speaking quietly. "Emery," she said, "I need some help for a change. I want to talk to somebody who shipped in on the *Bolivar* this morning."

"The *Bolivar?* Let me see now." Emery pulled out a heavy black book from the shelf under the desk. He opened it near the middle and ran a stubby finger down the list of names. He looked up at Chris. "Yes," he said. "We have a man here named, he says, Davy Jones." Emery made a face that indicated he had at least one Davy Jones around all the time.

"Can you get him down here?" Chris asked.

Emery closed the book and slid it back on the shelf. "Take a seat in there," he said pointing to a sitting room off the lobby. "I'll see what I can do."

Chris turned away from the desk and walked into the lounge. It was empty except for a long-legged young merchant marine who sat at a table in the corner laboriously writing a letter.

Chris sat down in a huge leather arm chair and took out a cigarette. She leaned back and relaxed, sending a stream of smoke toward the ceiling.

For a minute she watched the young sailor nibble dolefully on the end of a wooden pen. Then her eyes moved upward to the shelf over his head and the model of a whaler under full sail. It was so perfectly done that she could see the belaying pin in the minute hand of a minute gob.

She heard the sound of heavy footsteps in the hall. She looked up expectantly toward the doorway.

A giant of a man in a dirty T-shirt and bell-bottomed dungarees entered the room, paused for a moment at the door, then walked toward Chris. A tattoo of a naked woman with a snake wrapped around her neck peeked demurely through the thick black hair on one arm, like a mermaid playing it coy behind a lattice of seaweed.

He stopped in front of Chris and stood towering over her. "Lookin' for me?" he said. She could hear the roar of the sea in his big booming voice.

"You're Davy Jones?"

"Yeah."

"I understand you shipped on the *Bolivar*," Chris said.

"Yeah," he said.

"I'd like to ask you a couple of questions," Chris said.

Davy gave a short nod. He sat down in a straight-backed chair facing Chris. The chair was too dainty for his bulk. He shifted uncomfortably, then spread his knees and leaned his hands on them.

"First off," Chris said, "was a man by the name of Max Petersen on board?"

Davy grinned broadly. "The rummy, you mean," he said. "Yeah, he was there."

Chris stubbed out the cigarette and looked back at Davy. "Fine," she said. "I hear the ship ran into trouble."

"Yeah," Davy said. "Blew a boiler. Hell of a mess."

"And that you put into an island to make repairs," Chris continued.

Davy nodded. "Tongariva," he said. "Stinkin' little place with bugs. No Dorothy Lamours, nothin'. Stinkin' little place with bugs." He shrugged and spread his hands in obvious disgust.

Chris smiled. She knew exactly how he felt. She'd realized on her first trip to the islands that they forgot to put the bugs and the heat and the dysentery in the movies. And the closest thing she had seen to a hula girl was a saggy old dame with the itch.

"Did you get down to the lagoon?" Chris said. "Max tells me it's a good place for swimming."

"Swimmin'!" Davy snorted. "What would that rummy know about swimmin'? Nah, I never got there. I was stoker on the ship, ma'am. I stood over the boiler like she was a baby. But I heard some of the other guys talkin' about it. Like swimmin' in a bathtub of boilin' water, they said."

"Did you happen to hear anything about the shells in the lagoon?" Chris asked.

Davy frowned. "Well, some of the guys were lookin' for pearls. Didn't hear of anybody findin' nothin' though."

"That's all?"

"Yeah," Davy said. "That's all."

Chris nodded. "Thanks," she said.

"For what?" Davy said.

"You've told me what I wanted to know," Chris said. She turned and walked toward the door.

Davy stood looking after her. He shrugged.

At the corner Chris stopped another cab and headed uptown.

She knew now that at least a good part of Max's story was true. He had been to Tongariva and there was a lagoon, whether Max had seen it or not. That still didn't tell her whether she would find a Glory there, but it was a start.

Only one thing bothered her now: the shell

around the native's neck. Chris could think of at least a dozen reasons why Max hadn't been able to bring it back. But she could think of an even better reason why he would risk anything to do so. A perfect Glory-of-the-Seas, like the one Max described, would bring up to fifteen hundred dollars if one had connections. Max had a connection. And if he'd brought that shell back with him, Chris wanted to get her hands on it. What better proof could Jonathan ask for?

The shabby little shop on Third Avenue looked like anything but a thriving business. A crack ran diagonally across the window. It had been taped up a long time ago with a promise to be fixed; it never would be. Behind the glass thousands of shells, conchs and panamas and cochinas and cones had been dumped in around a giant clam. A heavy layer of dust, apparently never disturbed, mantled and mellowed the display.

Chris opened the door and went in. The tinkle of a bell brought a pasty-faced man out of the back room. He looked to be the shabby owner of a shabby shop. Yet Chris knew this gentleman must be worth a considerable fortune. He'd been on the shady side of the law all his life. He specialized in smuggled pearls, but he'd been known on occasion to do some fancy trading in valuable shells.

Chris knew that if Max had brought back the Glory, he would have come here with it first thing, even before he got in touch with Jonathan. Jonathan wouldn't dream of offering for it what Tritt could raise on the closed market. For Tritt dealt not with museums, but with private collectors who could afford to pay a scalper's price for a rare item.

"Mr. Tritt," Chris said. She turned on a friendly smile. She did not like Mr. Tritt.

"What can I do for you, Miss Hamilton?" Mr. Tritt took off his glasses and polished them with the hem of his coat.

"I'm not sure," Chris answered. "I'm looking for a couple of things you probably haven't got."

"Oh? Like what?"

"Well, for one, like a Glory-of-the-Seas," Chris answered. "Brandt's trying to pick one up for the museum. I thought you'd be able to get hold of one, if anybody could."

Mr. Tritt adjusted the spectacles on his nose. "You flatter me," he said. "I've never seen one. And I haven't heard of one being up for sale since Chappell died."

Chris picked up a shiny cone shell off the counter and turned it over in her fingers. "We'd be willing to pay up to twenty-five hundred," she said.

Mr. Tritt sighed. "I'd be willing to take it," he said. "But I haven't got one."

"And you wouldn't know where to get one?" Chris said.

"No," he answered. "I wouldn't know where to get one."

Chris put down the shell. "Okay," she said. "But let us know if you should hear of anything."

Back on the street Chris headed for the nearest candy store.

She'd have to take Tritt's word about the shell. She didn't dare let him get too suspicious. If he knew Max was in town and offered Max enough cash, Max might just forget where his loyalties belonged and give Tritt the whole story. Tritt wasn't above sending out a diver of his own, if he thought he could make a profit. The way he worked, he'd probably clear a thousand a shell and then beat it before anybody got wise.

It would have made things a lot easier to have gone to Jonathan with proof. He wouldn't like the idea of sending an expedition on a wild shell chase. But Chris knew that, somehow or other, she'd talk Jonathan into letting her go. This was a chance too good to miss.

She dialed "Information" and got the number of *Marine Life*. Then she put through a call to Mr. Peale and negotiated a deal. He agreed to take a series of three articles, with photographs in color. Five thousand for the lot.

Chris grinned as she hung up the phone. Nothing like being mercenary while you're having the time of your life.

And now she'd better get up to the museum.

10

For an hour Chris talked without letting Jonathan interrupt. She glanced at him occasionally to check his reaction. But mostly she let herself be carried away by her own excitement, striding the length of the office and back again, speaking with her hands and her heart.

When she had finished, Chris stopped pacing and came to sit on the edge of Jonathan's desk. She looked down at him and said, "And that's the whole story. Max didn't see the shells himself. We don't know if there's anything to it. But if there is . . ." She spread her fingers on her lap.

"Um hmm," Jonathan murmured. "We've got a corner on the market." His eyes narrowed shrewdly. "Current asking price is about a thousand per. Even two or three hundred wouldn't bring it down too far. Half maybe." He picked up a pencil and did some rapid calculations on a scratch pad. He looked pleased with the result.

"Jonathan," Chris said, "please forgive me for sounding pedantic. But in the interests of science, do you think we could afford to keep one for the museum?"

He looked at her and smiled. "Chris," he said, "you misjudge me. I have every intention of keeping the finest specimens of anything I can get my hands on for this museum. But don't forget," he peered intently, "it will take cash to finance this trip and to pay you. I can't afford to be too idealistic."

Chris snorted. "Heaven forbid you should get idealistic, Jonathan. But I didn't mean to be sarcastic," she said hastily. "My only interest in getting those shells is the fact that they are rare and they are beautiful. I keep forgetting you're a businessman."

She knew better than to be too hard on Jonathan. He had to clear his every move with the Board. And the Board didn't know from sea shells, only from dollars and cents. The Board didn't care about beautiful and rare and prestige. It wanted only that Jonathan get the most with the least.

Chris slid off the desk and stood up. "Well, how about it?"

Jonathan brought his hands together on the desk

90

and stared at them thoughtfully. "One more thing," he said. "Or rather two. First, why were there no shells washed up on the shore?"

"I've been thinking about that too," Chris admitted. "The live ones, of course, would be in the water. But it's only sensible to presume that some of them die off. There should be a couple on shore. But then there's the business of the breakwater." She paused to consider. "It's possible that the tide coming through isn't strong enough to drag them in past the coral and the rocks. I expect the shells would've settled into crevices and pockets. It's not impossible."

Jonathan nodded, satisfied. "All right," he said. "Now this: why only one shell on one native? And why didn't Max bring back that shell, since you've proved that he didn't?"

"Well, like Max said to me," Chris answered, "the snails aren't edible and the natives are too practical and too lazy to bother diving for something they can't eat. They haven't got supermarkets, you know. Anyhow, it's possible some of the other young bucks use them for decoration. He didn't take a survey."

Chris knew that her argument was not very convincing and that Max's bloodshot eyes would have spotted any Glory on the island. She could only hope that Jonathan was intrigued enough, as she was, to take a long chance on a little evidence.

"Perhaps," Jonathan said dubiously. "But why didn't he pick up that one?"

Chris smiled. "I see you don't know those islands, Jonathan," she said. "Or Max. You don't take anything personal, even an adornment, from an islander. He's still primitive enough to believe you're going to hex him, and savage enough to have no qualms about a little thing like murder. There's always a chance you'll find a non-believer who'll barter with you. But Max rarely has anything more than the shirt on his back." She laughed. "When I saw him, he didn't even have that."

"He's got five hundred dollars," Jonathan said.

"That's now."

Jonathan sighed and leaned back in his chair. "I can see you've made up your mind to go," he said. From his tone Chris knew that Jonathan would back her up with the Board.

"Yes," Chris said. "I have."

"Very well, then." He pulled open the middle drawer of the desk and extracted a long black check book. "I'll get busy first thing in the morning. You'll work with Miss Martin on the details."

"Fine," Chris said. "May I use your phone?"

"Of course."

Chris picked up the phone and dialed home. Dizz caught it on the second ring.

"Hi, Dizz," Chris said. "Good news, darling. I've got a job."

"Oh?" Dizz answered. "Going fishing, dear?"

Chris wanted to reach out and slug Dizz when she got like that. But she kept her voice steady.

"Don't be funny," Chris said. "I'll tell you when I get home. In about an hour."

"Well, please be sober when you get here," Dizz said. "George will be dropping by this evening."

Chris wanted to say he should drop dead, but checked it. She felt her enthusiasm begin to wane. "Okay," she said and cradled the receiver. She frowned and made a fist with one hand and hit it lightly against the desk.

"Anything wrong?" Jonathan asked. He was holding a check toward her.

She took the check, folded it and slid it into her pocket with the one from *Marine Life.*

She shook a no. "Everything's fine," she said. "Dizz's a little worried about my diving again. It's been almost two years."

"Perhaps she's right to be," Jonathan said. "I wish you'd make a few trials before you go off to Tongariva."

"I might just do that," Chris answered. She started toward the doorway. "See you tomorrow."

"Yes," he said.

Chris left the office and walked across the long hallway and through the display rooms toward the solarium out back.

She cursed herself silently for having let Jonathan see her discomfort with Dizz. Even though he had introduced them, he had obviously been hoping for years that it wouldn't last between them. Not that Dizz would give him a tumble — she found the pudgy little gentleman extremely irritating. But simply that nobody else should possess her either, since he realized that he could not.

Chris rapped lightly on the side of the arch.

Carol turned quickly from the counter. She looked at Chris without saying a word, her eyes and her smile bright with pleasure.

"Hi," Chris said. "I didn't have a dime to call, so I thought I'd drop by instead." She crossed the room and leaned against the counter beside the girl.

"Liar," Carol grinned. "I saw you going into Dr. Brandt's office ages ago. I thought you'd gone home by now."

93

"Without saying hello?" Chris smiled back at her. "Don't be ridiculous, darling." She took Carol's hand and squeezed it affectionately.

Carol slid off the stool and crossed to a small table in the corner. "Coffee?" she asked.

"Sure," Chris said. She moved to the stool and sat watching Carol. She found herself fascinated by the way the thighs moved beneath the skirt. There was something intriguingly feline about the movement, something smooth and lithe, yet strong. She felt a shiver of excitement run up her spine, an urge to reach out and touch.

Easy, girl, Chris told herself. What the devil would Jonathan think if he walked in here and found you pawing Carol. Not that it matters what Jonathan thinks. But what might he tell Dizz?

Chris folded her hands in her lap and pressed her thumbs together hard. She forced her eyes upward and away from danger.

Carol took a glass pot from a two-burner stove. She carried it into the lavatory and turned on the tap. In a moment she returned with the pot full and set it on the burner.

"I heard through the grapevine that Max Petersen's back in town," Carol said. She put two cups on the table, ladled in instant coffee and sugar. "Has that got anything to do with your being here?"

"Do you know Max?" Chris asked.

"Only by reputation," Carol answered. "He wrote most of the textbooks I used at school. Why?"

"Just curious. He's been out of the business for years."

Carol lifted the pot off the stove and filled the

cups. She added a shot of milk to each. Then she carried both cups to the desk.

"Come sit over here," Carol said.

Chris got off the stool and walked to the desk. She pulled forward a straight-backed chair and sat down.

"Well, I'm waiting," Carol said.

Chris took a sip of coffee, then leaned back against the chair. "Well, it's a little vague at this point. But Max claims to have found what he calls hundreds of Glory-of-the-Seas shells off the coast of a South Pacific island, Tongariva. We haven't got anything but his word to go on." She paused to reflect on that for a minute, then added, "But he's never been known to be wrong, so we're taking a chance on it."

"You're going?" Carol asked.

"Right. I wouldn't miss a chance like this if I had to finance it myself," Chris said.

Carol leaned forward excitedly. "Darling, that's wonderful," she said. "I know you must be thrilled."

What was it Dizz had said? "Going fishing, dear?" Oh, my poor darling beloved Dizz, Chris thought. Why don't you understand? Why do you always have the wrong word to say about everything? Always the one that hurts? Why?

To Carol she said simply, "I am."

"When are you leaving?" Carol asked.

Chris thoughtfully ran her fingers through her dark black hair. "Brandt'll arrange most of the details. I expect I'll be able to leave by next weekend. He has, by the way, assigned you to help me with the incidentals," she said. "We'll have to dig up all

95

the info we can on this place. Like if there's edible food and water to drink. And tides and water temperature this time of year. You know, the works."

"Good," Carol said. "When do we start?"

"Tomorrow morning."

They sat for a few minutes in silence, each taking an occasional sip of coffee.

In the back of her mind Chris was seeing this gorgeous little girl in bed, naked and reaching out her arms to be loved. It was a sweet picture. Carol who cared and wanted her. Not like Dizz. Not like Dizz who could knock the excitement and joy and pleasure right out of her and leave her alone and frightened. And she knew that she needed Carol to care and to want her. Maybe not forever like she needed Dizz. But at least for now.

"Carol," Chris said, "do you think I could persuade you to spend the weekend with me?" She hadn't prepared the speech. It found words of its own.

Carol laughed. "What makes you think you have to persuade?" she said.

Chris flushed. "Darling, you shock me," she said. "I haven't made any definite plans yet. But there are two things I want to do before I take off on this trip."

"Like what?"

"Well, for one thing, I would like to do some diving before I get to Tongariva. I had a rather bad accident a couple of years ago. You've seen the scar on my thigh. And I haven't been diving since." She shivered at the memory of it and of the horror that gripped her every time the memory came back.

"Hmm, yes," Carol said. "I remember reading

about it in the paper when it happened. And what's the second thing?"

Chris leaned forward and looked intently into Carol's eyes. "I'll probably be away for a month or more," she said seriously. "And before I go, darling, I'd like to get to know you a little better. I find," she smiled, "that I'm developing a definite weakness for you." It sounded corny, she knew. But she couldn't say, "I love you." It wasn't true. And Dizz had taught her never to say, "I need you."

"Well," Carol said, "thank heaven for that."

"I'll have to see what I can arrange," Chris said. "Dizz usually doesn't want anything to do with these jaunts. But she might get perverse." She stared thoughtfully at the cup, then lifted it and drank the last few drops.

It would be just like Dizz to foul up the works, Chris thought. But I can't let her do it this time. Carol has something I need. And I want it.

"Where would you like to go, if you can arrange it?" Carol asked.

Chris rose and stood looking down at Carol. "I think," she said, "the Inlet would be a good place."

"You'll freeze."

"Nope. I've got one of those rubber suits like the frogmen wear. I've been swimming off Nova Scotia in it." Chris smiled. "Besides, I'd like you to see where I grew up."

"Good," Carol said. "I'll see you in the morning then?"

"Right," Chris said. "And if you should happen to see me with a cigarette, old girl, please take it away from me, will you? I've got to build up a little wind power in a hurry."

Chris started toward the archway, then turned to face Carol. "I think we'll have a lot of fun working out the details on this Tongariva business," she said. "But let me warn you right now. I'm a pretty tough boss — a pain about little things. After all, a lot depends on the information we find out."

"Like your life," Carol said quietly. "I know."

Chris waved goodbye and started for the street door.

She was elated at the idea of a weekend with Carol. She had had one sharp pang of guilt, but she had fast talked herself out of it. After all, she told herself, it was Dizz who sent me out that first time. Its not like I'm being unfaithful. It's just that I'm doing the only thing I know how to do. The way Dizz told me to do.

And for the moment Chris almost had herself convinced that it was her right to have someone who could give her the affection Dizz could not. Not for one second did it occur to her that Carol could ever replace Dizz in her life. Simply that her frustrations could find a release with her.

She could wait until tomorrow to start worrying about Tongariva. But right now she had to figure a way around Dizz for this weekend.

11

Dizz was in a rage which, apparently, she had been working on all day. Not a screaming rage. Dizz never screamed. But sullen, silent and decidedly unfriendly.

Chris tried for an hour. She told Dizz about Max and about the shells and about Jonathan. She talked on happily about the importance of the find and her own joy at the part she was going to play in making it. She was excited and the more she talked, the more excited she became.

And Dizz listened. Or at least seemed to. She had

nothing to say. There was an expression on her face that clearly said she couldn't be less interested.

Chris saw the expression and she felt her hands grow cold and the heart go dead within her. She never expected Dizz to take an interest in her work nor to offer encouragement. But she could say something. Anything. She didn't have to sit there and look at her like she wished Chris would just go away.

Damn it, Chris thought. You've been much too sweet the past couple of days, my girl. And I, wistful fool that I am, forgot for a while. I must be getting soft in the brain.

Chris poured herself a second cup of coffee. She sat stirring it slowly. She could think of nothing more to say.

"Are you quite finished, Chris?" Dizz said icily.

Chris did not look up. "Yes," she said, "I'm quite finished, Dizz." Her voice was dead. Her enthusiasm over the trip, over life, over living, over anything she'd ever been happy about sneaked off into a corner and died.

"Then let me get the dishes cleared up," Dizz said. "George will be here early."

Chris picked up the cup of coffee and carried it with her to her bedroom. She closed the door quietly and went to sit at the desk. She pulled out a drawer, propped her feet on it and leaned back in the chair. She stared at the wall in front of her. She did not see it or anything else.

She wanted desperately to think about Carol, about the weekend and Tongariva. She wanted to think about anything but Dizz.

But no matter where she searched in her mind, it was always Dizz she found there. Dizz, whom she'd held last night and loved. And with whom she had failed. Dizz whom she loved and beside whom a career and Carol and everything else mattered not at all. She wanted Dizz to care, to shout and rage if necessary, but not to sit there, bored and annoyed. Not to dismiss her. Not to say, get up and go away. I can't stand you.

Oh, Dizz, her soul cried out, what have I done wrong now?

Or maybe it wasn't she this time. Maybe Dizz'd had a spat with Georgie boy. She must have talked to him today. That's it. It's not me. It's that damned George. She doesn't care about me. It's George.

Sure — she's afraid that George is angry at her and won't care about her. She's afraid that he won't want to climb into bed with her anymore.

Well, don't worry, kid. No man in the world ever looked at you without getting hot. No man ever looked at that body without wanting to climb all over it. George'll take one look at you, and that's it. And you'll probably let him. The hell with me. The hell with us. You like George today. You don't want him to be mad at you. And if he touches you —

By the pernicious route of abject self-pity, Chris managed swiftly to work herself into a state of complete depression. She did not shift her position. She stared bleakly in front of her and saw nothing. After a while she was not even thinking. She was numb.

Dimly, from miles away, she heard the buzzer ring in the kitchen. Still she did not move. She wanted no part of George. She wanted to be alone with her misery, did not want George to see the tears at the edge of her eyes or know by the quiver in her voice

101

that she had given up. She did not want him to realize that she knew he could pick Dizz up and run away with her.

Dizz did not come to call her. She could hear them out there, talking and laughing now and then.

Laughing at me, probably, Chris thought. Poor dear fool who gets all excited about a sea shell. Poor dear fool. Poor fool.

She began to see pictures in her mind. Pictures of George taking Dizz in his arms. Kissing her, caressing her. Whispering to her and loving her. Dizz — her girl.

Then other pictures, a whole procession of them. A movie, sort of, in technicolor. Not to mention stereophonic sound. She was stalking George across an island jungle, driving him to the sea — driving him into her element where she could catch and kill him. And somewhere, in a secret cave, was Dizz, waiting to be rescued. And the tide was coming in and the water rising and in ten minutes Dizz would be drowned. She had to hurry and . . .

At the hottest point of the chase, a knock sounded at the bedroom door. Chris tumbled back to reality; the hot-blooded hero sat up abruptly. She braced her hands against the desk, her arms stiff in front of her.

"Chris," Dizz called. "May I come in?"

"Of course," Chris answered.

Dizz opened the door and walked in and across to sit on the bed. There was something very deliberate in her movements and something very deliberate on her face.

Chris looked past her to the living room. There was no one there. "Where's George?" she said.

"I sent him home," Dizz said. "I told him I had to talk to you about something."

"Oh?" Chris felt her eyebrows rise toward her hairline.

Dizz propped her elbows on one knee and leaned her chin on her fist. "I don't quite know how to say this, Chris," she began. "But I have to find out."

"Darling, there is no reason why you can't say whatever's on your mind." Chris felt little of the confidence she displayed. She had the terrible feeling that Dizz was going to tell her something about George and herself, something that would leave Chris alone and out of it. Maybe they were already having an affair. Maybe Dizz wanted to marry him.

"Well," Dizz said, "Jonathan called back right after you left. He wanted to talk to me. You know what an old maid he is," she said, a little apologetically.

In a flash of understanding Chris knew what was coming — Jonathan was still out to break them up and would use any method he could find. No wonder he'd been so generous with Carol's time. Chris braced herself.

"Anyhow," Dizz went on, "he said, you know, that he didn't want to start anything. But he thought I should know that you spent yesterday afternoon with his new assistant, whom he describes as a gorgeous brunette."

"So?" Chris said casually. She did not feel casual. The hair on her scalp prickled and the palms of her hands were suddenly damp.

Dizz hesitated. "I wouldn't have given it a second thought," she said. "Except that you got home pretty late last night, plastered and ashamed of yourself."

Chris waited, sitting very still.

"Darling," Dizz said slowly, "I know you're not always happy with me. I knew it last night. I felt you crying. I have a fairly good idea of what you do on weekends. I can't really blame you. And I can accept it." She looked down at the floor. "But the idea of you getting serious about someone else just never occurred to me before. I don't like it."

Chris felt the tension relax and she settled more comfortably into the chair. She wouldn't know what to do if Dizz wanted to leave her. But if all that bothered Dizz was that Chris might be taking off, well . . .

Chris' hearty laugh betokened infinite relief. "Is that all that's eating you?" she said.

"Isn't it enough?" Dizz said with annoyance. She was not taking the situation lightly.

"Look," Chris said seriously, "let me set you straight about something. I'm in love with you, Dizz. Four years more so than the night I met you. I still flip every time I look at you. Nobody, but nobody does to me what you do. And don't forget it." She said it with all the sincerity in her and she knew that it was so.

Dizz looked at her sharply. "And what does this Carol Martin do for you?"

Chris was silent for a long minute. Then she said, "Let me put it to you this way. Carol is a marine biologist. She understands when I get elated over a sea shell. That's the only thing she's got over you."

Dizz cocked her head on one side and thought it over carefully. She gave no indication of understanding or of belief.

"Will you be seeing a lot of her?" Dizz said.

104

"I'll be working with her pretty closely until I leave for Tongariva," Chris answered.

"Is she going with you?"

"Of course not," Chris said. She was getting irritable. Not because Dizz did not believe her so much as the fact that she would not let it drop. Dizz would believe whatever she wanted to, regardless of the truth. But Chris, with a sense of guilt teasing her, could think of no words to make Dizz be still.

Dizz sat still, frowning to herself. "Chris," she said, not looking at her, "do you love this girl?"

Chris thought it over carefully. She did not want to lie to Dizz. Dizz would know if she did. At the moment she could safely say that she was not in love with Carol. Just deeply fond of her. But, despite what she believed to be her undying love for Dizz, Chris could not promise that her feelings for Carol would not grow beyond fondness.

For Chris was wise enough to know that it was possible for her to love them both and at the same time. One of them desperately and without hope, the other constructively and with shared enjoyment. She did not care to contemplate what would happen if the time came for her to make a choice. For the moment, she was not ready to part with either. Carol, because she offered tenderness and affection and understanding. And Dizz — well, just because she was Dizz.

She decided to take an indirect tack.

"Dizz," she said, "do you know that while you were out there with George, I was sitting in here driving myself mad? I was sick with jealousy and fear. And when you came in, I thought you were going to say you're eloping with him or something." It hurt

105

her to admit it, to let Dizz see behind it. But she could think of no other way out.

Dizz laughed as heartily as Chris had a few minutes before. "You ninny," she said. "George is just a friend. I enjoy him, that's all."

Chris grinned. "See what I mean?"

"What?" Dizz said, looking puzzled. Then the face relaxed. "Oh," she said.

Chris got off the chair and squatted down before Dizz. She took both the girl's hands in her own. "Honey," she said, "I'm repeating myself, but I love you. You're a part of me, like my hair on an arm. I wouldn't be complete without either. Or without you." She kissed the curled fingers. "And if you ever hear me cry, it's not because you don't make me happy. It's because I haven't done the same for you."

They were quiet together for a long time, with their hands clinging. Chris saw in Dizz's eyes something close to tenderness. It had been many heartaches ago since Dizz had looked at her like that. And many tears.

Finally Dizz said, "You won't leave me?"

Chris sighed. "No," she said. "I won't leave you." And if I could believe that you would keep that glow, she thought, I would never even look at anyone else.

Dizz stood up. With a finger she tousled Chris' hair. "Shall we drink to that?" she said. "I could use one."

"Sure," Chris answered. "I'll take coffee, though. No more alcohol or cigarettes till I get back from Tongariva."

Dizz fixed herself a drink and got coffee for Chris. She came back to the bedroom and put both drinks on the desk. She sat down on the chair.

Chris had sprawled out on the bed and lay with her hands linked behind her head. She was relaxed now, the pieces of her world all back in place. She was ready to believe they could go on together forever, as they had always gone on, and that nothing could interfere.

"How long will you be gone?" Dizz asked.

"A month. Maybe more."

"Chris," Dizz said, "tell me honestly. Will this be a dangerous job? I can't help remembering the last one."

"I thought we settled all that this morning," Chris smiled. "It could be, of course. Any diving job could be. I prefer to consider the cheerier aspects."

"I know," Dizz said. "But how do you think I feel, sitting here for a month? Not knowing whether you'll be coming home in one piece or ten — or none."

Chris nodded. "You're right," she said. "You can always come along, you know."

"This may be the shock of your life, my dear, but I have every intention of doing just that," Dizz said triumphantly.

"Do you mean that?" Chris said, afraid to believe it.

"I do," she said. "No gorgeous brunette is going to know more about this trip than I do!"

"Ouch," Chris said. "I thought you were afraid I'd drown."

Dizz picked up her glass and drained it in three long swallows. "I believe in killing two birds with every stone," she said.

At the mention of the gorgeous brunette, Chris remembered her proposal to Carol. Somehow it all seemed very far away and just not very vital. Dizz was going to Tongariva with her. The first time since that trip to Nova Scotia. Maybe, alone and away from the city, they could get a new start together, work out some of their mutual disappointments. If it could be again like it was that first night, the hell with sea shells. And with Carol.

But she had promised. And she knew Carol loved her. And she needed the trip anyway. And . . . And if she didn't go, Chris told herself, she might spend the rest of her life wondering about what she could have had with Carol. Learning to resent Dizz, even to hate her, when she climbed into her solitary bed and slept her lonely sleep. Wondering till the day she died if it wouldn't have worked out better with Carol.

Chris remembered painfully the hideous result of last night's attempt with Dizz. And the bitterness she held in her heart. And the softness and the sweetness of Carol. She knew she had to find out.

"Honey," Chris said, "I thought I'd take a trip down to the Inlet this weekend while you're off seeing your family. I want to see if I still know how to swim."

"Will you need any help?" Dizz asked.

"Not really. It would be fun to have you along. But it's probably the last chance you'll have to go home for awhile." Oh, Chris, she thought, you're such a shrewdie.

"That's right. I hadn't thought of that," Dizz admitted. "I guess I can trust you for a weekend. How are you going?"

"I thought I'd rent a car," Chris said. "That's the easiest way."

"I'll ask George if you can borrow his. I don't think he'd mind," Dizz said.

Chris did not protest. Things were confused enough without adding to it.

"Well, I'm going to bed," Dizz said, getting up and starting for the door. "We didn't get much sleep last night."

Chris blew her a kiss. "Good night," she said.

Dizz paused just outside the door. "Chris," she said, the old ice creeping back into her voice. "I didn't mean to get sloppily sentimental awhile ago. I've always told you that you were free to leave at any time."

"Forget it," Chris said. She knew the disappointment was audible. She had enjoyed the moment's delusion of foreverness. But Dizz didn't know the word.

Chris got up from the bed and picked up the cup of coffee. It was cold. She put it down.

Somehow, she thought, it would straighten out. She could work something out with Carol. And Dizz. It would have to be all right with Dizz. She needed Dizz more than she would ever need anything else.

12

Chris walked through the archway and into the solarium. She snapped on the lamp hanging on a cord above the desk and threw her jacket over the back of a chair.

It was just before nine, Saturday morning. Carol had not yet arrived. Considering the fact that they had been working fourteen hours a day, Chris was not surprised. She'd had trouble waking up herself.

She sat down at her desk and pulled over a thick folder of notes. Inside she found the checklist of data to be gathered. She read carefully through the list,

checking off each item already covered. Everything was in order.

In three days she and Carol and the public library had amassed enough information to write a guide book to Tongariva and the Pacific islands in general. On Monday morning Jonathan would be expecting their report. He had taken care of the sea plane and diving equipment and clearance for the expedition. He'd spent a lot of money and he wasn't especially happy about it. Chris knew that her end of the deal had to be perfect.

Chris was satisfied that she and Carol had done a superior job. And glad there was little left to be done today. She was tired to death.

Not only had she been working hard. She had been under an emotional strain that kept her from sleep when she finally crawled into bed.

Carol had proved to be little short of perfection as a co-worker. They had exchanged few words during the long hours, and then their talk was strictly business. Both had been completely absorbed in the job at hand. Yet just when Chris found her head throbbing and her back beginning to ache, Carol was there with coffee and sandwiches and a smile.

Dizz had proved to be decidedly less cooperative. It was something beyond the usual chameleon moodiness. Chris had long since grown accustomed to the flickering warmth that changed abruptly back to the more usual chill of boredom and disinterest. But during these past three nights had been added a subtle flavoring of disgust and contempt that Chris had not known before.

Dizz did not believe that Chris was working until midnight. She hadn't said that is so many words —

she wouldn't — but there was no warm supper when Chris got home; there wasn't even much pretense at civility. Dizz simply sat there on the couch, cold and serene, watching Chris, smoking, not saying a word. She had not been drinking. She was, indeed, sternly sober. And watching.

She was not listening when Chris spoke to her. She was not talking. And the one time Chris had made a move to kiss her, she had turned away in revulsion.

Alone and miserable in her bed, Chris had stared blankly at the ceiling until dawn came, until the alarm rang. And when she dared think at all, it was simply to pray that she could hold Dizz until they got away together. She dared not think that she could not win Dizz back.

And somehow it had gotten to be Saturday. In a half dozen hours she and Carol would be on their way to the Inlet in George's car. Dizz would bring the car around and leave her the keys. Not that she had said so — she had left a note on the kitchen table.

Chris heard the door close way out front and looked up, waiting for Carol to come into the room.

"Hi," Carol said, hurrying in and dropping her purse and gloves on the desk. "I didn't hear the alarm." She smiled at Chris and blew her a kiss.

"I gather," Chris said. "But I won't scold you."

Carol went quickly to the little burner and busied herself with making coffee.

"I haven't had breakfast yet," Carol said. "Have you?"

"No," Chris admitted. "I'll treat you to a big spread on the way down." She sighed and turned away from Carol. She did not want the girl to see the weariness and the strain.

"Honey, is anything wrong? You sound awful," Carol said. She was looking at Chris with genuine concern.

"Of course not," Chris said harshly.

"Well, excuse me, lady," Carol mocked. "I didn't mean to step on your corns."

Chris got up from the chair and crossed to stand and stare out the windows. It looked so peaceful out there in the tiny yard — the cold red bricks and the bare bleak maple, an old barrel and three paint cans with pink and yellow drippings. Nothing moving. No people. No women. No noise. Quiet, like at the bottom of the sea. It would be good to feel it again, the serenity and the peace of that quiet world.

Carol carried two cups to the desk and set them down. "Coffee," she said.

Chris drew a deep breath and straightened her sagging shoulders. She stepped over to the desk but did not sit down. "Carol," she said, "how do you feel about Dizz?"

"Frankly?"

"Frankly."

"From what I can gather that she's done to you, I could very easily despise her," Carol said. "But I accept her, like sort of a necessary evil. Because, though it kills me to admit it, I'm afraid she's got you pretty well hooked. Why did you ask?"

"You'll meet her today. She's bringing the car around." Chris frowned. "What makes you think she's got me so well hooked?" She felt hooked. But she didn't like the idea that Carol knew it.

Carol laughed. "Are you kidding?" she said. "But

seriously, darling. Just the way you look in the morning, before you get down to work. The sadness and the misery. But I can't feel too sorry for you. If you didn't like it, you would have done something about it long before this."

Chris did not answer for several minutes. "It sounds lousy," she said. She knew what Carol said was true, but it hurt to admit it.

"Can you deny it?"

"I don't want to think about it," Chris answered. "We've got work to do."

For three hours they worked. It was just a matter of getting the data in order and adding a couple of maps. There was nothing missing, absolutely nothing. They knew everything about that island. Except —

"Well," Chris said, "all we need now is a pile of Glories."

She dropped the folder on the desk and turned to beam at Carol. "Thanks, kid. You've done a good job."

"Thank you, darling," Carol said. "It's been my pleasure."

In her enthusiasm Chris stepped forward and put her hands under Carol's elbows and lifted the girl high into the air. She pulled her close and kissed her quickly on the lips.

From the doorway an amused voice solemnly breathed, "Well!"

Chris very gently lowered Carol's feet to the floor. Both turned in the direction of the voice.

"I do hope I'm not intruding," Dizz said. She was smirking broadly.

"Of course not," Chris said. "Come on in, Dizz,

this is Carol Martin." She nodded toward Carol. "Carol, Sheila Dizendorf."

Dizz stood aloof, calmly observing Chris' discomfort. In a powder blue suit and short coat to match, her hair blown soft by a brisk wind and her cheeks flushed pink, Dizz had never been more beautiful, nor more perfectly composed. She was, as always, master of the situation.

Carol was the first to move. She appeared completely relaxed and she smiled warmly at Dizz, waving her to a chair. Chris knew it was all a surface calm, but she approved. Dizz had a way of making her fizzle and die out. She felt something close to admiration for Carol for keeping her poise.

"Sit down," Carol said. "I was just going to fix some coffee."

Dizz crossed to a chair and sat down stiffly. She glared at Chris. "Thank you, Miss Martin," she said.

"Please call me Carol. Though I don't know how I'll ever remember to say Sheila," Carol said. "Chris mentions you a thousand times a day, but it's always Dizz."

"Yes," Dizz said haughtily. "She has some peculiar habits."

"But I think it's adorable," Carol blurted.

"So I gather," Dizz boomed.

Chris turned her head quickly to hide the smile. She sat down on the stool and swivelled to watch the two women. She felt like she was about to see somebody tossed to the lions. And she had the uneasy feeling she would be the person.

Dizz took a key in a leather case from her pocket and dropped it on the desk. "The car's parked out front," she said to Chris. "The black Thunderbird. All your gear's in the trunk. George helped me. I packed a basket of lunch and the big thermos of coffee."

Chris nodded. "Good," she said. "Did you bring my pea jacket?"

"Of course."

Carol put a cup of coffee, a container of sugar and a pint of milk on the desk beside Dizz. Then she carried a cup over to the counter.

"I hope I didn't put in too much milk," she said.

"No," Chris said. "It's fine."

Dizz raised an amused eyebrow.

Carol sat down near Dizz. Both of them looked straight ahead at Chris.

Chris shifted uncomfortably on the stool.

There was a dreadful silence in the room. Then, one by one, each found a moment's comfort in a coffee cup.

"Chris," Dizz said finally, "when shall I expect you back?"

"Monday about noon, I think," Chris said. "I plan to drive back at night. And since I have to see Jonathan at nine, I'll probably come directly here."

Chris watched Dizz glance aside at Carol. Carol was looking at Chris, smiling fondly.

"Yes," Dizz said. "I see. In that case I think I'll stay over at home till Monday morning."

Chris had the creepy feeling that Dizz did see, all too well. She searched for words to set things right.

"And as soon as I get everything set up here, I'll rush home," Chris said. "I'm dead tired now and it'll be worse by Monday."

Dizz remained serene. "You probably won't get much sleep," she said.

116

Chris ran her long fingers through her hair. She wanted to reach out and shake Dizz. To knock that complacent look off her face. Bad enough to have a guilty conscience without having to stand that cold, disdainful air.

Carol stood up and picked up the folder. She opened the top drawer and slid the folder inside. She closed the drawer and turned to face Chris.

"Well, boss," she said, "if we're through for the day, I've got things to do." Her eyes were tender. She looked to Chris like somebody who'd just heaved a life line to a drowning man.

"If you wait a few minutes, I'll drop you off," Chris said.

"No, thanks," Carol answered. "I've got some shopping to do downtown."

Dizz did not move. The look on her face was one of frank suspicion.

Chris helped Carol into her jacket and patted her on the shoulder. "See you Monday," she said.

Carol said her goodbyes and left the two of them alone. Neither spoke until the front door had slammed behind Carol.

"She's very attractive," Dizz said.

"Yes, she is," Chris said. "Is that what made you so friendly?" She was angry and she knew Dizz would hear it.

Dizz hesitated before she answered. Then she tilted her head and smiled that beguiling pussy cat smile. She stepped close to Chris and ran her long nails up the back of the girl's neck and into her hair. She pulled Chris' face down to her own and playfully traced the tip of Chris' nose with hers.

Chris shivered and pulled Dizz into her arms. She

117

pressed her lips into the warm hollow of the girl's throat and with her tongue caressed it.

Dizz gasped and moved tight against Chris, their thighs hugging.

"Chris," Dizz whispered hoarsely, "we're in full view of the whole world."

"Uh huh," Chris murmured. "Worried?" She knew it could be unpleasant if anyone saw them. But she was much too engrossed to care.

"Yes," Dizz said. "You work here." She moved away from Chris. "I'll be waiting for you when you get home."

"That's a promise?"

"That's a promise."

Together they put away coffee cups and closed up the office for the weekend. They went out through the display rooms and into the hall.

"Shall I drive you out to Queens?" Chris asked.

"No, honey," Dizz said. "I'm meeting my brother at his place. I'll take a cab."

"Need any money?"

Dizz shook her head. "No. I've got plenty," she said. "And darling, I'm sorry about Carol. I've been doing some off-color thinking lately."

"You've managed to convey that impression," Chris said. "As I said, she's just a friend."

"That's a promise?"

Chris laughed. "That's a promise."

Chris hailed a cab and saw Dizz safely inside. "Monday noon," she said. She gave Dizz a kiss and shut the door.

Dizz turned to wave as Chris ran across in front of a bus and leaped for the curb.

Two minutes later Chris nosed the car into the

line of traffic, then turned east toward First Avenue. Somewhere in the back of her mind she knew that everything was all wrong. She could not believe that they'd really put something over on Dizz. Not Dizz.

By the time she reached Seventy-second Street, Chris had already worked up a good case of nerves. This weekend with Carol would be a pleasure. But what in the name of heaven would she find when she got back home?

13

It was just before nine when Chris turned off on a narrow dirt road and began following it along the edge of a small but exquisite lake. On the far side, evergreens stretched for miles in either direction and in the broad expanse only the asphalt snaking up the hill and over the top marred the perfect blanket of blue green. There were no sails on the lake now, only a few tiny yachts bobbing tiredly at anchor, waiting to be put to bed for the winter. And everywhere there was a deep contented silence.

Chris drove into a rectangle of parking lot, empty

now except for the battered Ford station wagon she knew was Johnnie's, and pulled up close to the entrance. She leaned over and gently shook Carol's arm.

"Honey," she said. "We're here."

Carol smiled sleepily and put her head on Chris' shoulder. "I'll be here in a minute," she said. She yawned and patted her mouth daintily with three fingers. "Pardon me," she said.

Chris laughed and bent her head to kiss the girl's nose.

The door on Chris' side of the car jerked violently open. "Chris, you old devil," a great voice boomed. "Good to see you."

Chris turned quickly and began pumping a hand. "Johnnie," she said happily. "How've you been?"

Carol looked past Chris to the figure beyond. Except for the lights blinking down at the pier, she might easily have mistaken it for a big black bear. It was immense, up and down and across, and more arms than anything else.

Johnnie stooped low and peered into the car at Carol. "Hi," he said, then looked at Chris. "What happened to the blonde you were living with?" He grinned at Chris. There was no malice in Johnnie, Chris knew. Just plain honesty and not too much brains.

"She's at home," Chris answered. "Shut up and make yourself useful. There are two bags in the trunk." She handed Johnnie the keys.

Chris got out and opened the door for Carol.

"Chris," Carol whispered, "what's that?"

"Johnnie?" Chris laughed. "We grew up together. We were the scourge of Sussex County."

"I can well imagine," Carol said. "Between you, you must have ruined half the girls in the state."

Chris led Carol down a path to what had once been a boat house. The better part of the building was set out over the water on stilts. Inside there was one huge living and dining room, where a fieldstone fireplace threw off heat and light, and a small lobby with a flight of wooden steps leading to the second floor.

"Johnnie's father used to build boats here," Chris said. "After he died, Johnny turned it into a fishing lodge. Does good business during the season."

Johnnie followed them in and started up the steps with the grips. "Cook's got dinner on," he said. "We saved you a couple of big lobsters."

"Fine," Chris said. She followed Carol in to stand by the fireplace.

"This makes me sleepy all over again," Carol said, wiggling her fingers into the warmth.

"Never fear. We'll get to bed as soon as we've eaten," Chris said. She herself was almost asleep on her feet. And she could not afford to be tired tomorrow. She needed all the strength she could muster.

In a few minutes Johnnie came to join them. On close inspection one realized that the man was well over six feet tall and as homely a man as Chris was handsome a woman. He had a great mass of fire red hair and shockingly black eyes that never lost their good-natured smile. He looked like fun.

"Chris, you damn fool, are you going diving this time of year?" he asked. "I saw the stuff in the trunk."

"Yes," Chris said. "I've done worse things."

"Don't brag about it," Johnnie said. "Frankly, the water's been pretty rough the past week or so. Been a lot of off shore storms." He was obviously concerned.

"Look, I promise I'll be careful," Chris said.

"Just in case, kid, we still following the old rules?" Johnnie looked at Carol and winked.

Chris burst out laughing. "That's up to the lady," she said.

"What did he mean?" Carol asked when Johnnie had left them to check on dinner.

"Johnnie used to get all my old girls when we were in high school. He never made out too well with that mug of his," Chris said.

"I like him," Carol said.

Chris nodded. "So do I."

All through dinner Chris kept smiling to herself. She was remembering fondly the good days when she and big Johnnie were kids. Long before they realized that there were women in the world. When there were just the two of them. Pals. Johnnie had been Chris' hero. They had had good times together.

Like the time they'd run away from home together and decided to be hoboes on the beach and live on seaweed and fish. They'd built a fire on the sand that night out of driftwood and weeds. They'd dug up a dozen clams and put them on hot rocks to bake, and Chris had taken her fishing pole and gone down to stand in the surf and cast. The next thing she knew, Chris found herself fighting the pole and being dragged out to sea. She'd yelled and big Johnnie had run and grabbed the pole away from her. It was only a small sand shark, but even big Johnnie had to fight for twenty minutes to beach him.

123

And Johnnie hadn't laughed at her; just asked if she was okay. It was like Johnnie was her big brother.

It had always been like that for them. Until they grew up a little. Handsome young woman Chris could get the girls ugly young man Johnnie wanted. Johnnie couldn't get anybody till Chris was finished. And then it wasn't big Johnnie anymore — then it was Chris who was boss.

Chris sighed. It had been fun to have a hero. The best thing about being a kid.

Carol let her eat in silence, knowing her thoughts were years away.

Johnnie joined them again after dinner. He was carrying a bottle of wine and three glasses.

"I saved this for you, kid, for next time you came. May wine," he said. "Nobody ever asks for it but us." He poured three glasses. "A toast. To a beautiful lady," he said, bowing to Carol.

"I thought you were off alcohol," Carol said to Chris.

"This is a special occasion," Chris answered.

"Please go easy on it."

"Right," Chris smiled.

Johnnie got up and went to the radio and turned on some soft dance music.

"May I have the first dance?" Johnnie said to Carol, bowing from the waist. He looked like a big buffoon, but one you couldn't help but love.

Carol blushed. "Certainly," she said.

Chris sat watching them. She was annoyed and, on two glasses of wine, already a little tipsy. She was annoyed with Johnnie for dancing with her girl, holding her too close and pressing his lips to the top of Carol's head. She was annoyed with Carol for enjoying it. And she was annoyed with herself for not doing something about it.

For several minutes she held back, knowing Johnnie would not dare make a pass at any girl and certainly not one who belonged to Chris. But she could not bear the way Carol relaxed against Johnnie, the way she was dancing with her eyes closed and smiling. She realized it meant nothing, no threat to her. But they looked good together and it irritated her.

She got up and went unsteadily to cut in. She put a hand heavily on Johnnie's shoulder. "Shove off, mate," she said. "I'm not dead yet."

Johnnie released the girl. "Sorry, skipper," he said.

Chris took Carol in her arms and stood holding the girl tight against her. They swayed to the rhythm.

"Darling, you didn't have to be so nasty," Carol said.

"Look, you're my girl," Chris said angrily.

"You're jealous?"

"So I'm jealous," Chris said. "So what?"

Carol stepped back and looked at her. "And just how do you think I feel about Dizz? Having to lie and sneak around. Do you think I like that?"

Johnnie sat watching them.

"Keep your voice down," Chris said. "You'll bring the fire engines." Her irritation showed in her tone. She didn't like having her private life aired in public. And at the moment even Johnnie felt like public.

Carol touched her hand. "I'm sorry, honey," she said softly. "It's just so silly for you to be jealous. You know I'm in love with you."

Chris pulled the girl close again. "Let's go upstairs," she said. "I've got things to say to you."

Chris settled the bill with Johnnie, in case he wasn't up when they took off. She wanted to get started early to catch low tide.

"Take my card," Johnnie said to Carol. "You might want to come back sometime."

Chris led Carol upstairs to a large wood-paneled room. The ceiling-to-floor windows faced over the lake. There was a fire in the grate and the room was warmly cozy. The blankets had been turned back on the bed.

"It's so beautiful," Carol breathed. She was standing by the windows gazing out to the lake.

"Yes, isn't it?" Chris said, coming to stand behind the girl.

They stood together looking at the night. Chris put her arms around Carol's waist and Carol leaned back against her. They did not move nor speak for many minutes.

"Honey," Carol said finally, "does Dizz know we're together?"

Chris pulled the girl closer against her. "Why do we have to keep talking about Dizz?" she said. "We came here to be away from all that for a while."

"You didn't answer my question," Carol said.

Chris turned away from the girl and went to sit on the edge of the bed. Her jaw was set in anger. "I think she guessed," she said. "What difference does it make?"

"Look," Carol said, coming to stand in front of

her. "I want to say something to you. After this, I'll never mention it again. But please hear me out."

Chris gave a resigned sigh. "Get it over with." She was in no mood for a scene, but too tired to fight it.

"I have to admit that this morning's episode upset me terribly," Carol said. "I had managed somehow to forget that Dizz exists as a person. But seeing her this morning reminded me with a jolt." She paused. "And having to lie to cover up for us — well, that wasn't quite what I'd had in mind."

"Nobody asked you to," Chris pointed out to her.

"I did it to save your face," Carol said sharply. "Oh, Chris," her voice softened, "don't you understand? I love you with all my heart. I want you. But I want to have you all to myself. Dizz, even if it doesn't show, actually wants the same thing. You've hurt her, even if you're too thick to see it."

Chris wrinkled her forehead. "What do you mean?"

"You have given her a kind of security these past years. Do you think she's happy that she can't give you what you need? Don't you realize that she has no real basis for security with anyone?" Carol was exasperated. "Darling," she said, "I just don't know how to fight somebody who has nothing to fight with."

Chris shook her head sadly. "What, for Pete's sake, are you trying to say?"

"I don't know myself," Carol answered. "I guess I'm trying to say that you've got to make peace with yourself about Dizz. And soon. If you're going to live with her, then you'll have to stop seeing me. She couldn't bear the thought of you having a mistress.

That would make her as good as useless. And I won't tolerate sneaking around behind her back. I love you too much to let you do that because after a while you would come to hate me for it. And yourself."

"What do you want me to do?" Chris asked.

"Whatever will make you happy," Carol said. "Go back to Dizz or come home with me."

Chris looked at her. "Is that an ultimatum?" she said.

Carol hesitated just long enough to make Chris uneasy. Then she said, "No. A suggestion." She put her hands on Chris' shoulders. "Now, let's forget everything but us."

Chris smiled wanly and realized how sober she was again. "I'll try," she said. She reached up and grasped Carol by the arms and pulled her on the bed on top of her.

Carol tenderly touched the eyes, the nose, the chin, the mouth with her lips. "We've got a big day tomorrow, honey," she said. "We'd better get to bed."

"That's one reason," Chris laughed.

There was a series of muffled raps at the door.

"Damn," Chris said. She kissed Carol lightly and rolled out from under her.

Chris opened the door to find Johnnie standing there with a pot of coffee and cups on a tray.

"Thought you might like some coffee, kid," Johnnie said. "I know how you are about it."

"Thanks, Johnnie," Chris said, taking the tray. "I'm sorry I barked at you awhile ago, mate."

"Sure, skipper," Johnnie said.

Chris closed the door with her foot and carried the tray to the bedside table. She looked down at

Carol. She couldn't have been less interested in coffee.

"I don't want to sound morbid," Chris said. "But if anything should go wrong tomorrow, call Johnnie. He always knows how to handle trouble."

"I'll remember that," Carol said. "But if you drown, I'll never forgive you."

Chris lay down on the bed and pulled the girl to her. "Shut up, will you? If there's anything I can't stand, it's a lot of talk."

They didn't talk again that night.

14

It was shortly after six when Chris turned off the highway just short of the bridge. She pulled up in front of a ramshackle building with the legend LUNCH–BAIT on an equally ramshackle sign above its roof. A trickle of smoke lazed upward from a stovepipe at the back. A gull perched on the edge of a creel, jabbing its beak through the cracks. There was no other sign of life.

"We can get breakfast here," Chris said. She got out and came around to open the door for Carol. "Place belongs to Clem Saunders. He used to be a sea captain, he says. I think he had a tug or something."

Carol followed Chris into the shack. They sat down at a three-legged table covered with well-worn red and white checkered oilcloth. There were three other tables in the room and a six-foot counter with stools.

Chris tilted her chair back and let out a bellow in the direction of a curtained doorway. "Clem!"

Nobody answered.

"He's probably out catching some bait," Chris said.

"Well, you have to eat something," Carol said. "We'll just have to wait."

"Wait, nothing," Chris said.

She got up from the chair and went around behind the counter. She opened the door of a wooden icebox and peered inside. She pulled out four fish patties and slapped them on the grill. She added six strips of bacon. She set a half dozen eggs on the counter and slammed the ice box door.

"Scrambled," she said. "That's all I know how to fix." She broke the eggs into a bowl, added milk, salt and catsup and whipped vigorously. Then she dumped the contents of the bowl onto the grill and stirred it with a fork. She picked up a spatula and flipped the fish cakes, then set the bacon to drain on a paper towel.

Carol came to join her behind the counter. She set out two plates, then carried silver and two mugs of coffee to the table.

Chris slid the fish cakes, bacon and eggs onto the plates.

"You look like an old hand at that," Carol said.

Chris grinned. "Sure," she said. "Johnnie and I used to work here during the summers. It's the only greasy spoon in miles."

Chris set the plates on the table and sat down.

"You must be handy to have around the house," Carol said.

"Ha!" Chris said. "Dizz says I'm a monster. She won't let me near the kitchen. I wash dishes backwards, she says. I don't even boil water to suit her." She went at the food with vigor.

When they had finished eating Carol looked up at Chris coyly and said, "What does she like about you?"

"Let's not get started on that again," Chris said. The last thing she wanted from Carol this morning was another lecture.

"All right," Carol said. "But you started it."

Chris was about to answer when the outside door banged open. They both turned quickly to face it.

A five-foot spider of a man in a hat, a slicker and hip boots stood poised on the steps, a bushel of paper shell crabs hefted up to his knee. He was looking at Chris and beaming toothlessly.

He shoved the basket into the room and trotted across the floor. He jabbed out a skinny claw of a hand.

Chris grabbed the hand and shook it hard. "Clem," she said, "you get handsomer every day."

Clem let out a cackle and slapped Chris heartily on the back. "Thankee, Chris," he lisped. "Glad to see ye made yerself to home."

"Clem, this is Carol Martin," Chris said, smiling at Carol.

Clem lifted his hat, then jammed it back on his

head. He winked at Chris. "A pretty one, Chris," he said. "A right pretty one. You ain't changed a bit, I see."

Carol laughed. "Thank you, sir," she said sweetly.

The grizzled face grinned. Clem bowed stiffly, then turned to Chris. "You seen Johnnie yet? He's allus askin' about ye," he said.

"Yes. We stayed over there last night," Chris answered. "I always get in touch with Johnnie when I'm down this way. But tell me, Clem — how's the tide running this morning? I aim to take a swim."

Clem frowned and clicked his tongue. "Yer a crazy kid, Chris," he said. "Ain't nobody but a damn fool would be goin' in that water today. Runnin' high the past week. Current's wild. Ol' Neptune's been spewin' his guts all over the beach. Never seen so much driftwood and stuff." He looked a little frantic about it, like it wasn't good for his rheumatism or maybe even his soul.

Chris took a gulp of the hot coffee. "I need practice," she said. "I've got a big job coming up and I've been loafing for the past two years. What can I do?"

Clem turned and spat a brown stream of tobacco juice into the bait basket. He pushed his hat back on his head and scratched where the hair used to be. "Best to go back to the bay, fer's I can see," he said.

"Nope," Chris said. "That's like diving for sharks in a goldfish bowl. I need to feel the water trying to break me."

"Chris," Carol said. "Maybe he's right. It might not be safe." She put her hand on Chris' arm and looked pleadingly into her eyes.

Chris sighed. She had been counting on Carol to

133

give her moral support, at least to behave as though she believed in her.

"Look," Chris said, "the day I have to do my diving in the bay is the day I quit. You can stay here with Clem if you're scared."

Carol shrugged. "You're the boss," she said. But her eyes said, "Please don't go."

Chris pushed back her chair and stood up. "Let's go, then," she said. She turned to Clem. "What do I owe you, old timer?"

"Looks like I oughta owe you," he said. "You done all the work. Let's make it on the house."

Chris grinned. "Right," she said. "I'll let you know if I drown."

"Ye don't need to do that, youngster," he said. "I'll hear this one," he nodded at Carol, "hollerin'." He looked at Carol and winked broadly.

Clem walked with them to the door and stood looking after them, running his eyes over Carol's trim shape. He clucked approval then turned back to the basket of bait.

Chris took Carol by the hand and led her over the sand to the bridge. They stood leaning on the railing, looking down at the swirling water below. The tide was out now, but the water stood high against the marker. It was murky black and it looked as if it would freeze the hide off a polar bear.

They crossed back to the car and got in.

"He's right, you know," Carol said.

Chris did not answer. She started the engine, then swung back to the highway. She turned left.

"You're going anyhow?" Carol said.

"Yes," Chris said. "I'm going anyhow. Don't you understand? I have to."

134

"What are you trying to prove, Chris?" Carol said. "Has anyone ever accused you of being a coward?"

Chris banged her fist against the wheel. "That's not the point," she said. "I'm scared. Scared as hell. It's me I've got to show, not anybody else. I've been diving under worse conditions than this. I have to know I still can."

She knew she could not explain to Carol the demon that was driving her on. Ever since Johnnie's words of warning, it had been creeping up on her, the fear. But every inch of the way she was fighting it, struggling desperately to kill the urge to back out and run away. It was no longer a simple rational thing, a desire to dive just to prove she still could. It had become a need that must be met. She knew it would not kill her to try. She just had to prove that she had the guts to do it.

Chris swerved the Thunderbird onto a hardpacked sand trail that ran over the dunes. She stopped at the dunes at the head of the beach.

"There it is," she said. She looked ahead to the vast expanse of ocean and at the waves curling up the sand. After a long silence, she turned to Carol. "Still scared?" she said.

Carol laughed. "No," she said. "No little old ocean can polish off a blockhead like you."

Chris smiled. "That's better," she said. It helped, having Carol believe in her. It helped, having somebody waiting for you.

"Honey," Carol said.

"What?"

"Hold me a minute," Carol said.

Chris twisted from behind the wheel and took the girl in her arms. She pressed Carol's face against her neck and squeezed her face against the soft dark hair. The smell of perfume rose to her nostrils. Not sexy, like Dizz's, but as fresh and tangy as the ocean air. It did not drive her wild, like Dizz's. But she felt the stir of desire deep within her and she wanted to hold the girl and caress her.

Chris slipped her hand under the girl's coat, over her breast, then down to her waist. Carol moaned in her ear, pulled her face back and turned her lips pleadingly to Chris.

Chris grabbed Carol and kissed her hungrily, deeply. She pressed her body against Carol and they fell together against the door of the car.

"Darling," Carol crooned. "Love me, darling."

The throaty voice snapped Chris back to consciousness. She remembered what she was doing here and why she must make Carol wait.

"Not now, baby," Chris whispered. "I've got some business to attend to."

"I'm sorry, honey," Carol said. "I shouldn't have started it."

Chris sighed and disentangled herself. "But I'll see you later," she said.

"That I know," Carol said. "I've got the shakes now."

Chris opened the door behind Carol and both of them got out.

"I'll drag the gear down to the beach," Chris said. "You start gathering driftwood. I'll need a fire when I get out."

"Okay," Carol said. She turned and ran off down the beach.

Chris pulled the key out of the ignition and walked back to the trunk. She lifted the lid and propped it open. She took out the air tanks and set them on the sand.

Well, kid, she thought, this is it. In a half hour you'll be up to thirty feet over your head in sea water, out where nobody can see you or hear you or help you. What happens then? Do you lose your nerve and just stay down there? Or do you take a little swim and come back to shore?

She shuddered and turned her eyes again to the sea, her first and only enduring love. It rolled on, heedless of her and the terror inside her. It did not tremble in fear of mortal combat.

Slowly she climbed into the scuba suit. She carried the rest of the equipment down to the edge of the water and called to Carol to help her with the air tanks.

"There," Carol said, adjusting a strap and pulling it tighter. "You look just like a fish."

"Let's just hope I can swim like one," Chris said. "Wish me luck."

"I do, darling. But I don't think you'll need it."

"Hmm. But if I'm not back in fifty minutes," Chris said soberly, "drive back to Clem's place and call Johnnie. He'll know what to do."

If I'm not back in fifty minutes, Chris thought, neither Johnnie nor anybody else can help me. But it'll do both of us good if we can convince ourselves it isn't true.

"All right, honey. But you wouldn't do that," Carol teased. "You owe me something."

"Right," Chris smiled. "I do."

Chris kissed Carol tenderly on the lips, then turned away. She took a deep breath and said a silent prayer. Then she walked toward the waves.

137

15

Like an eerie monster from the murky depths, Chris went down to the sea.

She stopped knee-deep and bent to rinse the face plate of her mask in the water. In the rubber suit, the flippers, gloves and mask, she was completely covered. The tide was on the ebb. Water swirled around her, knocking her gently from side to side. But there were no waves breaking over her. And here on the shore, it was as quiet as a summer's morn. There was nothing sinister on the face of the ocean, certainly nothing to aggravate her fear.

She turned her eyes toward shore and saw Carol standing in the early morning mist, waving to her. Directly overhead and far back over the dunes the gulls were mewing and wheeling, searching for scraps. Carol had noticed them and for a second terror had shown in the lovely dark eyes. For gulls on shore meant one thing: rough water at sea. And rough water could play havoc with a diver, even one as experienced as Chris.

Chris raised a hand to Carol, then turned again to the ocean. She was about a hundred yards up from the mouth of the river. Even in a strong current, that was a pretty safe distance from the pilings which jutted far out into the deep, marking the mouth of the channel and the pathway up the river. She checked her position again and, satisfied, headed north, cutting across the current.

As she waded ahead, Chris had to admit to herself that she was afraid. She hadn't felt this way since that first time, so many years ago. Johnnie had been with her then and Johnnie had taught her how. He had led her down to the sea and taught her to swim with the fish. And it hadn't been long before she had left Johnnie far behind and headed alone for the deep water.

And she had done a lot of diving in her day, in places nobody else had dared to swim. She had grown confident and maybe just a little bit cocky. She had forgotten that the sea demands respect even from the creatures who roam its depths, and even more so from the ones to whom it did not give birth.

Chris knew, though she'd never said it even to Dizz, that her bout with the barracuda was no accident. It was plain carelessness. She'd been so

139

intent on finding a certain relic that she had forgotten to remain alert to danger. She had not kept an eye on her partner or seen him signal. And the barracuda had struck. If she had been alone that time, she wouldn't have come out alive.

Many a night that barracuda had cut across her dreams and brought her awake in a sweat. But she had learned her lesson. She had learned respect, and a caution that at the moment amounted to cold fear.

Chris knew that she had to put her fear where it belonged — behind her. She knew that she had to make this dive. If she couldn't do it today, she would never have the nerve to try it again. And once she was in the water she dared not be afraid. For fear could bring on cramps and panic. And panic meant certain death.

She set the mask carefully over her nose. She put the mouthpiece between her teeth and adjusted the line to the double tanks strapped to her back. She turned the valve on the right tank and tested it. She eased the canvas straps between her legs into a more comfortable position.

She stood poised on the outer edge of a sand bar. A foot in front of her the water dropped abruptly to a depth of twenty feet. She made a final check of her equipment.

She went over the edge feet first. And the instant she was submerged, she felt her body respond. The panic she had expected to seize and paralyze her did not appear.

Chris cut the water smartly and struck deep to the bottom. She swam clear of the bar and headed out to the open sea. She moved easily through the water, her eyes open, alert to her deep green world, her senses keenly alive to every sensation.

Below her fronds of eel grass sent up slippery fingers to catch at her and slide past. There were few fish now and only an occasional crab scuttling across the bottom. A sand shark lazed past, unconcerned with his weird companion. An eel slithered over her calf and wiggled away.

The element was alive and something infinitely more disturbing than fish or weeds. Bits of cork and tin cans and wood and shell and flotsam of every description, stirred up from the depths far out at sea and heaving in toward shore, whirling and eddying around her with each swell of the sea.

Exhilarated by her return to the great Atlantic, Chris soon relaxed and began to play and somersault, now racing a little green fish, now flipping over to float on her back. She was oblivious to the signs around her, heedless of danger and a stranger to fear. There was no trace of the nervousness that had consumed her for days. She felt only an overwhelming joy at being home.

She wished that Carol could be with her. It would be wonderful to cavort here with Carol, chasing and dodging, and even just looking, observing life here at the bottom of the sea. This you couldn't put in any museum. You had to see it first hand.

She remembered how it used to be with Johnnie, how the two of them used to dive together when all they had was a couple of pairs of homemade goggles. Then they used to pretend they were going to find a pirate's chest of gold or the hull of a sunken ship.

They learned over the years that there wasn't

much pirate's gold to be found off their tiny strip of coast and that the bottom of the sea wasn't littered with wrecks. They had learned the pleasure of playing tag with a blow fish, grabbing one and rubbing his belly to watch him bloat. And of finding a beautiful shell with the snail still inside and alive, not the dried out ugly husk they would find on the shore.

And she wished Carol could be here to see it all now. Carol would appreciate it. Not like Dizz, who would only run to the very edge of the waves and stick in a toe, never putting so much as a whole foot in the water. It would not be that way with Carol. She could teach Carol to be at home under the waves.

Diverted by her thoughts and by the scene around her, Chris was completely unprepared for trouble. She swam slowly, idling with the current, breathing easily and letting her body revel in the feel of the sea.

It was hardly ten minutes before she felt the first sharp pang of discomfort. On the swing up from an elaborate back bend, the left thigh convulsed in a sudden spasm, then relaxed.

It had been a full two years since that business off the Tortugas; as far as Chris had been aware, the leg had healed as good as new. There had been crutches and therapy and the doctor had pronounced her cured. But there it was — she could feel the twelve-inch scar etched in pain.

She swam slowly, favoring the leg. She sensed the weakness of it on the downward pull. She knew she was going lopsided and pulled hard with her arms to keep herself on an even keel.

There was a good three-quarters of an hour left in the tanks. Plenty of time to get ashore at a snail's pace; even before Carol had a chance to get worried.

As yet Chris was aware only of slight discomfort and the fact that it was not as easy to swim as it had been a few minutes before. But she was confident in her ability.

She changed her course and headed in. As she turned the second cramp hit. She winced with agony.

Slowed to a crawl and no longer intent on the mystery of this other world, Chris became conscious of something above and beyond the pain. She was cold, chilled through. She knew she was shivering. Numbness began to spread through her limbs like a creeping paralysis. There was a knot of muscles in her stomach that felt like a granite boulder pulling her down.

She figured herself to be about half a mile from land. That distance was like nothing — when you've got air and a good stroke.

Another dozen strokes. And another. This time the spasm came and stayed. The cramp did not relax. She tried to straighten out the leg. Nothing happened. The leg was bent nearly double and held as though in a vise.

The leg was useless to her now and she knew it. The pain was nearly intolerable. But somehow, she knew, she must not give in to it.

Her arms cut powerfully through the water. She tried feebly pushing with one leg, but that didn't help much. It seemed to be suffering sympathetically and didn't want to move.

She stopped shivering long enough to feel that she was beginning to gasp for air. With one tank gone, she had a half hour to make it, or . . .

For a second, panic gripped Chris. She saw herself doomed in her watery grave. But she was like a fish in water; it had been her natural habitat most of her life. And a fish doesn't drown. She was damned if she wouldn't put up a good fight.

Floating close to the bottom she managed to adjust the valve on the second tank. Her fingers were stiffening with the cold and the muscles in her arms ached. She knew she had more air left than strength.

Chris set herself a course for shore, cutting down toward the inlet and hoping to take advantage of the current's drag. With a little luck she would be able to make the line of pilings and follow them into shore. At worst she'd be swept into the channel and the river, where the pull of the water wasn't so devastating.

She found herself going full steam ahead and getting nowhere. Caught between the downstream current and the inexorable turning of the tide, every stroke carried her only inches toward her goal. She did not have power enough left in her arms to slice across the water's double drag.

She began to know a terrible fear, a more deadly chill inside than the one already numbing her limbs. Think of something pleasant, she told herself. Think of something pleasant. Think of Carol waiting on shore. Waiting to help you, waiting with a fire to warm your aching bones. Think of Carol.

For minutes at a time she let herself drift, being pulled by the conflicting forces almost parallel with the shore. Once she tried to surface, only to realize she hadn't strength left to pull out of the undertow.

But the force of the undertow meant that she was close to shore, too close to give up. Too close to die.

In a burst of energy born of fear, Chris surged ahead, stroking powerfully with her arms. She commanded her legs to begin the steady rhythmic beat that would get her home. The right leg moved.

She didn't know what happened with the left. It went back and out for the kick. Then it pulled up and caught in a final, hideous cramp. The pain shot through her hotly and brought tears to her eyes. Then she blacked out.

Ten seconds. Twenty. Thirty.

She hit the first of the pilings with a force that, on land, would have knocked the top of her head off. She took the blow on one shoulder. The blow jarred her awake and shook her the length of her body. She felt like she had been crushed by a falling tree. The rubber suit cut sharply across the barnacles on the post. They bit deep into her shoulder, grazed against the bone. Blood mingled with sea water, oozing out through the tear in the suit and trickling down her back.

In a daze she realized what had happened. And in a daze she became aware of her own blood in the water around her. Objectively she knew that the rubber suit had been torn and, apparently, her shoulder mangled. She felt the water seeping through the hole, running down her back and legs and filling up the feet and leggings of her suit.

Again and again she felt herself smashed against the pilings, too far gone to hold herself off or to grab on and hold fast. Her head, her hands, her shoulders crashed against the wood and the shells.

Minutes, torturing minutes, passed. She began to breathe slowly, steadily, getting a grip on herself and the situation. Finally she made a move. She grabbed hold of one of the pilings and grasped it with her arms and knees. She held on with one hand while she pulled off the flippers with the other. Then she put her arms around the next pole toward shore and let go with her knees. With each move the waves tore at her, pulling at her and nearly breaking her grip. But she hung on for her very life.

Like a starfish Chris clung to those pilings and made the final yards to shore. Inch by inch, her belly scraping across the barnacles, hanging by her fingers, ripping her gloves and fingers to shreds, she moved. Using muscles that felt already dead, she moved.

She did not know how many centuries it took her. Pyramids are younger than the centuries it took her. But it happened. She got there. She saw the misty morning and the beach and the dunes. She heard a sea gull.

And she heard Carol. Carol running along the sand, calling to her.

The last ten feet she made like a snail, creeping on her stomach, pushing with her hands when a wave rolled in and for a moment lifted her.

And then there was Carol, splashing through the surf and crying. Pulling her up onto the shore and all the while crying.

Carol kneeled beside Chris and loosened the straps of the tanks and pulled away the mask. She bent and kissed a bloody hand.

"Chris," she said, still crying, "Chris, darling, are you all right?"

Chris lay on her back looking up at the girl. She tried desperately to say that it was so. But she just couldn't make it.

"Get Johnnie," Chris whispered. Then she fainted.

16

The doctor had come and gone before Chris woke up.

She lay still on the bed, her eyes closed. Across the room she heard Carol and Johnnie talking in muffled whispers. She started to move and open her eyes, then relaxed against the bed. She had a lot of thinking to do before she let them know she was awake.

She knew the experience she had just undergone could make a lot of difference in her plans. Even now she realized that her confidence in herself had been badly shaken. Her work had been the one good thing in her life, her whole life except for Dizz. She didn't know anything else. And if she couldn't dive —

But she did not even know how to think in any other terms. Even since that first accident, she had not for a minute considered what she would do if she could no longer go out to sea. She had simply taken for granted that she would. And she would have to go on thinking that way.

The big thing, of course, was the Tongariva situation. From the way she felt now, Chris had a sneaking suspicion she wasn't going diving again for a long time. Every bone and muscle and pore of her screamed with pain. The leg lay stiff and cramped. She tried to move it. It didn't budge. The shoulder was heavily bandaged. Her fingers refused to bend.

She caught her lower lip in her teeth and bit down hard. It seemed somehow unjust. This should have been the trip to end all trips, the most important find ever. To have it snatched away, out of all reach — it just wasn't fair.

For a moment Chris considered the possibility of retribution. She had deliberately deceived Dizz. She had lied and cheated on her for years. She did not stop to question why the powers of justice should be backing Dizz. She suddenly believed only that she was being punished.

Yet Chris could not dwell long on defeat. Her scheme of living allowed no room for it. She had not time to lie here and feel contrite and sorry for herself. At nine tomorrow morning she had to see Jonathan. And after that? Well, after that, by heaven, she was going to Tongariva if she had to get there on crutches.

149

And she'd dive too. And swim. Only the good Lord knew how, but she was going to do it.

But first she had to get the hell out of this damn bed.

She opened her eyes. She realized that she was back in Johnnie's place, in the room she and Carol had occupied the night before. It was already twilight. There were no lights in the room except for the rosy glow of the fireplace. Long shadows crept across the floor and onto the bed.

Chris cleared her throat and tried to talk. All she could get out was a croak.

"Hi, skipper," Johnnie said. He stepped out of a dark corner and came to stand at the foot of the bed. "How's the kid?"

Chris tried again and this time managed. "I could use a drink," she said. She heard her voice come out hoarse and raspy.

"I figured as much," Carol laughed. She got up from a chair and stepped into the glow from the fireplace. She turned to a small coffee table, then came toward the bed with a bottle of brandy and a glass. "The doctor said it would be all right, though."

Carol poured three fingers of brandy and set the bottle down on the night table. She looked at Johnnie. "Lift her up," she said. "If she can take it."

Johnnie moved close to Chris and leaned over the bead. "Easy, kid," he said. With infinite care he slipped an arm under Chris' shoulders. Chris tried to put her arms around Johnnie's neck and found she couldn't move them that far. Johnnie easily lifted her to a sitting position.

Chris grimaced and felt the tears smart in her

eyes. Once she was propped up, it was better. Her rear end seemed to be the only part of her that hadn't been battered.

She reached out a hand for the glass. The fingers were stiff, like branches poking out from a tree. She could not bend them to grasp anything. She blinked her eyes to cut off a sudden rush of tears — she was beginning to feel sorry for herself.

Carol held the glass gently to her lips. Chris swallowed and felt the brandy burn a path to her stomach. She sighed and tried to manage a grin. It wasn't much of a success but Carol got the idea and smiled warmly in return.

"Well," Chris said, "I'm beginning to feel human again."

"Not so fast," Johnnie said. "You're entitled to sit still for a while, my friend." The look on his face meant that he intended for Chris to stay there for a long time.

"Like hell," Chris said. "I'm going to be in New York tomorrow at nine. Which means," she said, glancing at her watch, "we've got to get out of here by midnight. Six hours, mate."

"Chris," Carol said, "the doctor said that you're not to move out of that bed for at least a week." Her voice was gentle but firm. Chris snorted and shook her head. It hurt to move it but she didn't let anybody know it.

"Not likely, my dear," Chris replied. "A week from now I'll be in Tongariva."

Carol and Johnnie looked at each other across the bed. Johnnie lifted his shoulders helplessly. Carol bit her lower lip and turned away.

151

"Look, skipper," Johnnie said, "you're too big to hold down. And I know better than to try. But you're in no condition to go anywhere. Face it."

Chris gritted her teeth and set her jaw. She threw back the cover and swung her legs to the edge of the bed. She braced her feet against the floor and stood up, holding onto the headboard with one hand.

"Mate, you're a skeptic," she said. "I said I'm going back to New York tonight and I'm going back to New York tonight."

Johnnie moved forward to give her a hand. Chris found that she could not put her weight on the bruised left leg. She let Johnnie help her to a chair. Johnnie did not say anything, but his face was hard with disapproval.

Carol came and sat on the floor at Chris' feet. She cocked her head to one side and winked up at Chris. "You're crazy," she said. "But I love it."

Johnnie stood leaning against the mantle, hands in his trousers' pockets. His black eyes were almost somber. "Look," he said. "I ought to clobber you right now and throw you back in bed. But I won't. What I am going to do is drive you home. It's a long trip and you're not going to make it sitting up in the car. I've got an old mattress from a cot and a bunch of extra blankets. I'll fix up a bed in the back of the station wagon. Carol," he said, nodding at the girl, "can follow us in the car. Okay?"

Chris wrinkled her nose distastefully. She didn't enjoy being treated like an invalid. But Johnnie was right. The ache was too much. And maybe she could sleep. Maybe she could sleep enough to get the ache out of her by the time she saw Jonathan. He wouldn't be at all happy if he saw her like this.

"Okay," Chris said. "It's a deal."

"Good," Johnnie said. "I'll go get the wagon ready. We might as well get started as soon as possible." He started toward the door. "If there's anything you want, just send Carol down. I'll be out back."

When Johnnie had gone, Carol moved closer to Chris and leaned her head against Chris' knee. She looked up at Chris tenderly, her eyes soft with love. "Honey," she said, "what happened out there?"

"I got a cramp in this bum leg of mine, that's all," Chris said. "Johnnie and Clem were right about the rough water. Once I lost the use of my leg, I couldn't pull hard enough to get out of the current." She put out a hand and laid it on Carol's head. "I'm just thankful you were there when I got out. Otherwise I'd be fattening up the gulls by now." She rumpled the girl's hair affectionately.

"I told you you were too stubborn to kill," Carol said. "But what about the trip? Do you think you'll be ready to dive again that soon?"

Chris did not answer for a moment. She was ashamed to admit to Carol how she really felt. But she knew that Carol would guess, and that Carol had a pretty good idea of how badly she had been hurt. So she said, "I'm afraid I'll have to get Brandt to send somebody else with me. I won't miss this trip. But it's going to be a long time before this leg's going to get me anywhere. Not to mention the shoulder."

"I wish I could be with you," Carol said.

Chris smiled down at the girl. "Darling, I wish you could, too." She knew she meant it. Depressed, weary and sore as she was, Chris remembered just

153

two things — that Carol had saved her life, and that Dizz would give her hell for getting hurt.

Carol, her gentle Carol, would not yell at her. Not when she was beaten and miserable.

Too tired to think or care, Chris longed to lie in Carol's arms, to let Carol's tender touch and soft words ease the misery of her body and soul. She did not want to have to think anymore. Not about Dizz. Not about Tongariva. Not about anything. She wanted only to be held and loved.

She leaned forward and kissed the top of Carol's head. "Darling," she said, "I love you. And I need you, Carol. I need you to help me. I want to spend the rest of my life with you, like we are now, happy and alone."

Carol took Chris' hand and kissed the raw fingers. "Please be sure, honey," she said. "I don't want to lose you, once I think I've got you."

"You've got me, darling. I want to be with you. I want to put my head in your lap and go to sleep and sleep until it doesn't hurt anymore."

"I know, Chris. I know," Carol said.

"Oh, Carol, do you? Do you know I'm finished? That I'll never go diving again? Or chase off after a pearl or a treasure? Do you know?" Her voice was harsh with suffering. "I'll sit and write articles and limp around on a cane. I'll never get to Tongariva or anywhere else. I'm finished." She looked at Carol with something close to desperation.

"Honey," Carol said, "if I believed that, I'd shoot you now, like a race horse with a broken leg. For your own good." She touched the fingers again with her lips. "But you're going to see Dr. Brandt at nine. You're going to walk in there and tell that man you're going to Tongariva. And a week from now, as you said, you'll be there." She spoke with a conviction that did not sound forced.

Chris knew that it must be so.

They sat together in the dark, content not to talk. Carol sat leaning against the chair, her fingers around Chris' ankle. Chris brooded until, finally, she got bored with it. Then she began to plan.

The problem was first to get back on her feet. Then she could consider diving again. It wouldn't do much good to think about going to Tongariva if she couldn't even walk to the plane.

First you have to move all the movable parts. Like this, with the fingers. She got them into a claw, then relaxed. Then again. Now the leg.

Every movement was a torture. She wanted to scream, to let it out. But she flexed the fingers, then the leg. Then the shoulder, then the leg.

"Honey," Carol said suddenly. "What about Dizz?"

"What about her?" Chris said. She had managed not to think about Dizz for many minutes.

"Well, I'd like to have this week with you before you go."

"That's fair enough," Chris said.

"We'll have to tell her," Carol said.

Chris sighed. She did not relish the task. "I'll tell her myself. As soon as I get home tomorrow. It'll be better that way." She expected there would be a scene. No reason to put Carol in the middle of it.

Carol had had no part in the unhappy thing that had been her life with Dizz. No sense in exposing her to the bitter end of it.

"You're sure you want to do it alone?" Carol asked.

"Positive," Chris said. "I know Dizz."

They heard Johnnie come up the stairs and into the room. He was wearing a black pea jacket and carrying two extra ones over his arm. He handed one to Carol.

"Okay, skipper," Johnnie said. "I'm ready if you are."

"Right," Chris said. "I think you'd better help me, Johnnie."

Johnnie stepped to the chair as Carol scrambled out of the way. He helped Chris into the jacket and buttoned it for her. Then Johnnie lifted Chris in his arms like a child and carried her out of the room.

Carol switched off the light and followed them down the stairs.

When he had settled Chris comfortably in the back of the station wagon, Johnnie turned to Carol.

"We'll take it slow," Johnnie said. "We've got plenty of time."

Chris lay in the darkness. The voices moved off. She heard the mumble of them in the distance. She kept her eyes closed tight, her lips pressed together. She did not want to cry, and she was very close to it.

For some reason, everything seemed to have gone wrong with her world. Here she was, on the brink of the most important job she'd ever had, and she had gotten smashed up. And here she was, still in love with Dizz, and making plans to go off and live with another woman.

156

But I love Carol, she thought. She loves me and understands me and she'll help me pull myself together. Dizz wouldn't understand. All she'll have for me is an "I told you so." She'll despise me for being a failure. And Chris knew that nothing could hurt her more.

She heard Johnnie crunching over the gravel to the car.

"All set, skipper?" Johnnie asked, poking his head in the window.

"Yeah," Chris said. "All set."

17

Jonathan was having himself a quiet case of hysterics. He had been stamping up and down the office, chewing his nails and massaging his bald pate. Finally he sat down at his desk and made a meager attempt at self-control.

For two hours Chris had been patiently explaining to him that she was not about to die and was not even immobilized, and for two hours he'd been screaming that this was the most expensive and important project the museum had ever undertaken and that he could not risk sending her, that she was obviously in no condition to handle the job.

"All right," Chris said finally. "I'll make a compromise with you."

Jonathan stopped screaming. "For instance?" he said.

"For instance," Chris said, "you send Morris or Disney or somebody else along to help me. I'll let him do most of the dirty work. And take credit for whatever we find. I'll even finance my part of the expenses." It would be well worth it, even if she went a little hungry for awhile.

Jonathan frowned. "But why?" he said.

"Look, Jonathan," Chris said. "This trip means more to me now than finding Glories. It means my whole future. I have to prove to myself that I haven't been relegated to arm chair exploring."

Jonathan's eyes narrowed. "Are you afraid you might be?"

He had been waiting a long time for her to come a cropper, Chris knew, on account of Dizz. At the same time, he was not anxious to lose Chris as a scout for the museum. From the look on his face, Chris knew he could not decide whether to clap or weep.

Chris shook her head. "Not afraid, Jonathan. Just too block-headed to admit it."

"Well," he said, bringing his fingers together under his chin, "since you put it that way, I haven't much choice. But how do I know you're not going to take ridiculous risks? If anything happens to you, I'll get it in the neck."

"I'll swear to it," she said.

159

He sat pensively pursing his lips. Then he said, "Sheila's going to go with you, isn't she?"

Chris did not answer for a long minute. She knew what Jonathan had in mind. He would not trust her to behave, but he would trust Dizz to keep an eye on her. Dizz could be most adamant about a responsibility to anybody but Chris. She wanted others to think only the best of her. Chris guessed Dizz probably wanted her good opinion too. She just couldn't keep up the front all the time.

She thought of Carol and her promise to tell Dizz she was leaving her. Yet she knew that without Dizz, Jonathan could keep her from making this trip. And at the moment nothing was as important as this trip.

"Yes," she said. "She is."

"Yes," Jonathan said. "I think we can count on Sheila to keep you in line."

He came out from behind his chair and walked to where Chris sat. "You have everything in order, I trust."

"Naturally," Chris said. She handed him the heavy folder. "Look it over."

Jonathan was not satisfied until he had made a personal evaluation of every grain of sand on the island. He harangued over each minutest detail. Finally he closed the folder and clasped his hands on top of it. He looked across at Chris, a smile of approval in his eyes.

"Good," he said. "You'll leave the city Thursday at noon. We'll have a car here at eleven to take you and the others to the plane. We'll check on Wednesday for last minute items." He rose and leaned over the desk to shake Chris' hand. "Good hunting, Chris," he said.

"Thanks, Jonathan," she said.

Carol limped painfully from Jonathan's office, then stopped outside the door and leaned her back against the wall. Now that she was all clear with Jonathan, she had another problem on her hands.

What could she tell Carol to make her understand? Surely she must know how important this trip was to Chris.

But how could she know? Chris herself hadn't known until this morning. Lying awake on the mattress in the back of Johnnie's station wagon, she'd thought about nothing else the whole long way home. And she had lifted Dizz out of the framework of her plans and fitted Carol in. It would seem strange without Dizz, maybe even lonely for awhile. Dizz was not good for her, she knew. A life of self-denial and frustration, of self-abasement and of abuse was all she could hope for with Dizz. But there was a challenge there she would never have with Carol. The wish to possess something that would not be possessed, like chasing a butterfly that flitted always out of reach.

She and Carol could build something great together, working and playing and living together. A rich, constructive, satisfying life. Carol did not have the fatal fascination that belonged to Dizz. But she was gentle and good. She was beautiful and she could respond to passion, could feel desire and follow it to satisfaction. She would be good for Chris. They would be good for each other.

How can I tell her? How can I say, "I love you but you'll have to wait. I want to live with you, but I have something more important to do first."

Chris sighed and left her post against the wall.

161

She walked back to the solarium. She did not bother to knock, but entered and stopped just inside the door.

Carol and Johnnie were drinking coffee, nervous and waiting to hear from her.

"Hi," Chris said. "Johnnie, do me a favor and wait for me in the station wagon, will you? I want to talk to Carol." Her eyes were pleading.

"Sure, skipper," Johnnie said. He got up immediately and left the room.

Chris watched Johnnie leave, then turned to face Carol.

"Honey, what's wrong?" Carol said. "Did he say no?"

"Not quite. He made it conditional," Chris answered. She sat down in the chair Johnnie had just left. "I agreed to take another diver and put up the cash for my share." She frowned. She did not know how to phrase the rest.

"What else?" Carol asked quietly.

Chris flushed, knowing her discomfort was plain on her face. "He insists that Dizz go along as originally planned. He's always had a thing for Dizz. He trusts her more than he trusts me, anyhow."

Carol hesitated before she asked. "Did you agree?"

"Yes."

Carol got up from her chair and went to stand at the counter by the windows. She was crying almost silently.

Chris did not move. She did not have the words to comfort the girl. She could only wait until the hurt had passed and hope that Carol would forgive her.

After a few minutes Carol came to stand behind

Chris' chair. She put her cool hands on either side of Chris' neck and massaged with gentle fingers.

"Chris," she said, "I think I understand why you feel this trip is so vital." She paused. "At least I hope I understand. Anyhow, I know I have to trust you. I believe you love me and that you'll come to me when you can. In the meantime, I guess I'll just have to wait."

Chris reached up and took Carol's hands and kissed first one, then the other. "Thank you," she said. "I hoped you could understand. I don't know how valid it is, but right now Tongariva looks like heaven to me. I have to find out."

Carol returned to her chair. "Honey," she said, "will I be able to see you at all before you leave? It might be a couple of months before you get back."

"Hmm. I know," Chris said. She stopped to think about it. She knew that Dizz would blow her top one way or the other. Chris had promised not to leave her and Dizz would lash her with that promise like a whip. On the other hand, she probably suspected they had gone off together. Her pride alone should make her tell Chris to go. It would be easier if Dizz threw her out. Easier for both of them.

"I'll tell you what I'll do," Chris said. "I'll have it out with Dizz this afternoon. It has to be sooner or later, so why not now? I'll tell her I'm going to be with you until Thursday and that when we get back, I'll be living with you."

"She's not going to like that," Carol commented.

"She'll have to. I know what I want," Chris said, "and it's you. I'll be over sometime tonight." Her jaw was set with determination.

"Chris, darling. Please. Don't say it unless you're sure," Carol said. "I couldn't take it."

"I'll be there tonight," Chris said.

"I believe you," Carol said. "Because I love you."

"It's mutual," Chris said. She leaned forward and kissed Carol on the lips. "I'd better go now. Dizz said she'd be there at noon."

"All right, darling," Carol said. "Tonight." The word held promise of many things. And all of them were good.

Chris left Carol and crept painfully to the great hall. She stopped at the door and leaned her head against the cold wood. Her head was throbbing and her nerves were jangling. She knew she could not take much more.

Johnnie was waiting for her in the station wagon, listening to a ball game on the radio. He shut it off as Chris opened the door.

"What's up, skipper?"

Chris slid into the seat and slammed the door. She stuck out her lower lip and frowned. She did not know how to explain to Johnnie any more than she had known how to put it to Carol.

"I have to take Dizz with me to Tongariva," she said.

"The blonde?"

"Hmmm. The blonde. The boss man wants her to keep an eye on me," Chris said sourly. She turned on the bitterness as much to impress herself as Johnnie.

Johnnie turned in the seat and laid his arm along the back. "How about Carol?" he asked.

"I explained it to her," Chris said. "She says she understands. I'm going to try to spend the rest of the

164

week with her, then move in with her when I get back." She knew it didn't sound good. She would have laughed out loud if anybody had said it to her.

"You're going to tell blondie this?" Johnnie said.

"Yes, I'm going to tell blondie this," Chris said.

"Whew!" Johnnie said. He raised two fingers and gripped his nose. "That stinks. You think you've got trouble now. Just wait'll that dame gets through with you." He ran a finger from ear to ear across his throat.

Chris grinned sardonically.

"Look, skipper," Johnnie said, his tone serious and his eyes blacker than black. "I don't give a good damn if your girl blows you away. But I'd be awful angry, my friend, if anything happens to Carol."

Chris elevated an eyebrow. "Oh?" she said.

"Yeah, oh," Johnnie said. "I've got it pretty bad for her."

Chris nodded. She'd known that since she saw them dancing together. Johnnie, the big homely galoot, had given up to Carol without a fight. Johnnie, who'd never had a girl all to himself, had fallen for Carol and would do his best to protect the girl even from the skipper.

"Okay, mate," Chris said. "Let's shove off. By the way, you delivered the car, didn't you?" She'd promised Dizz to leave it at George's hotel.

"Sure."

"Did you find a place to stay?"

"Yeah," Johnnie answered. He was making no attempt to make light of the situation.

Johnnie made a U-turn and headed south on Fifth Avenue.

Chris did not try to break through Johnnie's reserve. He had right on his side and Chris was all too well aware of the fact.

And she knew too that if anything should go wrong this afternoon with Dizz, Johnnie would stand by Carol and help her get over the blow. She did not dare think of failure with Dizz, but it did help to know that Carol had someone to look after her.

"Look, Johnnie," Chris said. "Don't hit me. But do me a favor."

Johnnie glanced at her. "Carol?"

"Yes," Chris said. "Get in touch with her tonight. Just in case anything goes wrong with Dizz."

"I'm warning you, skipper," Johnnie said. "I love that kid."

"Yes, Johnnie, I know," Chris said.

"And I'm warning you something else," Johnnie said. "I'm not going to stand by and let you walk all over this one."

Chris winced at Johnnie's words. They were true, she knew. Until she had met Dizz, Chris had been a carefree, footloose devil. With a graceful ease that could charm the birds off the trees, Chris' life had been a series of one night stands. A whirlwind courtship, promises to be true forever, one lovely night, and off to the next one. And Johnnie, good old Johnnie, was left to pick up the pieces.

Not that Johnnie had ever complained. Envious of the way Chris had with women, he had stood by and watched with awe.

But not this time. Not with Carol. Because this time Johnnie really cared. This time he wasn't just being Chris' buddy. And at the moment he wasn't thinking much of Chris as a person either. That realization hurt Chris deeply.

Chris smiled sadly at Johnnie and nodded. "Okay, mate," she said. "I'll remember that."

18

Chris unlocked the door and walked into the apartment. Johnnie followed her in.

Dizz apparently had not been back to the apartment since she'd left on Saturday morning. It smelled stuffy and closed in.

Johnnie walked across the living room and pushed back the curtains. He opened the French doors.

"Nice place you have here," he said.

"We like it," Chris said. She went into the kitchen and managed to put up water to boil. She set out two cups and saucers and spoons. She had trouble with the lid on the coffee jar and swore.

When she returned to the living room, Johnnie was looking at a photograph of Dizz on the dresser in Chris' room. Chris heard him whistle.

"That's a good looking chick you've got," Johnnie said, coming into the room and facing Chris. "How do you manage?" He shook his head slowly in renewed admiration. Chris laughed.

Johnnie walked out to the kitchen. "Coffee black?" he said.

"Black."

They sat down together on the couch, drinking coffee and talking and laughing over the good old days.

At one point Chris glanced at her watch. It was after three. Dizz had promised to be home at noon.

"Excuse me," Chris said. "I have to make a call."

She went to the phone and dialed the Dizendorf's number. She asked for Sheila.

"Why, Chris," Mrs. Dizendorf said. "We haven't seen her all weekend. She said she was going away with you."

Chris did her best to cover up. Mrs. Dizendorf insisted on calling later to check up on Dizz.

Chris turned from the phone, her face a mask.

"What's the matter, skipper?" Johnnie said quietly.

"I'm not sure," Chris said. "But I think I'm being gotten even with." She sat down on the couch. "Dizz is playing games."

"What kind?" Johnnie asked.

"The usual routine. You run around behind my

169

back and I'll run around behind yours." It wasn't a usual routine for Dizz, but why bother Johnnie with her troubles.

"And you still care?"

"Yes," Chris said. "I still care."

For another hour Johnnie did his best to get Chris' mind off Dizz. With the wisdom of a brute, Johnnie knew that Carol wouldn't look at him twice with Chris around. But he wanted Carol to be happy, and if Chris could do it, then Chris was going to do it.

But Chris could not turn her thoughts away from Dizz. And she went from worried to scared to just plain furious. She kept an eye on her watch and one ear towards the door.

At four-thirty Chris heard a key in the lock. She was lying on the couch, feet propped up, her shirt open and the bandaged shoulder exposed.

The door opened and Dizz walked into the room. She took one look at Chris and exploded.

"What in the hell happened to you?" she shouted.

"Nothing much," Chris answered. "I'll tell you later."

Johnnie stretched up to six-three, then bowed from the waist. "Forgive me," he said. "But be good to the skipper. She's pretty beat up."

Dizz looked slowly from Chris to Johnnie and back to Chris. "Who," she said, "or what is that?" Her look was one of open and utter disgust.

"That's Johnnie Murdock," Chris said. "We went to school together. He was good enough to drive me home."

Johnnie shuffled uncomfortably, an alien in an

enemy camp. "Well," he said, "I'll be shoving off, skipper."

"Okay, Johnnie," Chris said. "And thanks."

Johnnie went out and closed the door behind him.

Dizz crossed to the sling chair and sat down. "Am I supposed to feel sorry for you? I told you this would happen." There was no indication in her manner that everything about herself was not just as it should be.

"Save your strength," Chris said. "It's nothing serious."

"What happened?" Dizz obviously did not particularly care what had happened. Her eyes were looking at Chris, but her thoughts were elsewhere. She didn't seem especially pleased with them.

"I got a cramp in my leg and got caught in the undertow," Chris said. She sat up on the edge of the couch and leaned forward, her arms on her knees. She took a deep breath, then jumped in with both feet. "Now, suppose you tell me where you've been."

"At mother's, of course."

"That's not what she says. According to her, you've been away with me," Chris said. "According to her, she hasn't seen you all weekend."

Dizz shrugged. "All right. I've been with George."

"Been where with George?" Chris asked.

"At his hotel," Dizz answered.

"And?"

"And what?" Dizz said.

"Did he make love to you?" Chris asked. She didn't want to hear the answer. She already knew.

"If that's what you call love," Dizz said. She looked as though she were about to be ill.

"He went to bed with you?"

"Yes," Dizz said coldly. "He went to bed with me."

Chris did something she had never believed she could do. She slapped Dizz in the face. Hit her hard. Again and again. And very hard.

Dizz did not try to stop her. She did not wince. She did not cry. She did not even yawn.

Chris grasped her hand and rocked in pain. The fingers were bleeding again. She pulled a handkerchief out of the pocket of her slacks and wound it around her fingers. She held the bandaged fingers tight in her other fist.

"Did that help?" Dizz said. Her eyes were icy blue and full of contempt. Her nose was tilted in scorn. And the corners of her mouth were raised in their perpetual smile.

Chris felt sick all over. Sick and tired and like running away. But she couldn't let it drop. She had to drain the situation of every last ugly drop.

"Is that all you have to say?" she asked.

"What do you want me to say?"

"Damn you, Dizz. Why did you do it?" Chris said.

"He asked me to marry him," Dizz said, as though that were excuse enough for anything.

Chris could not get out the question.

"I told him no," Dizz said in a flat tone. "Men are like Lesbians, only worse. I let him kiss me and all he wanted was to get my pants off. I let him do that too. What difference does it make?"

Dizz was talking as much to herself as to Chris. She had been disappointed again. And after disappointment came despair.

"I knew you were taking that girl with you," Dizz

172

went on. "I wanted to hurt you. What difference does it make?"

"Dizz," Chris said, "I love that girl. That's what difference it makes. I love her and I want to live with her. If I hadn't known it before, I'd certainly know it now."

Dizz glanced up for just a second. "You're going to punish me?" she said. "You? How many people have you slept with since we've been living together?"

"They weren't men, Dizz," Chris said. "I told you in the beginning I could take anything but that. I told you if you ever went to bed with a man, I'd never touch you again. That's what makes me sick."

Dizz did not look up. She said in a dull voice, "Leave me then. What difference does it make? I won't die."

Chris stood up. "I'm going to Carol's place," she said.

Dizz looked up at Chris finally, her face wet with tears. She was crying from deep inside, like a hurt child. She tried to speak but the words wouldn't come. She pulled herself from the chair and flung herself against Chris. Chris threw up her arms to ward her off, but too late.

They fell together to the couch. Chris' shoulder hit the wall and she groaned in pain. She fell back limply against the pillows, too agonized to move.

Dizz knelt at her feet, her head in Chris' lap. Her body was shaking with sobs torn from deep within her.

Chris pushed herself forward and bent low over Dizz, smoothing the girls' hair with her hand. "Baby," she crooned, "baby, don't cry."

173

Dizz looked up into her face. She gasped, trying to choke back the tears.

Chris put her stiff, sore hands under Dizz's arms and lifted her up. She pulled Dizz on top of her and stretched out on the couch. She put her arms around Dizz and held the blonde head close to her own.

"Honey," Dizz stuttered, "I-I-I love you."

Chris felt the tears start in her own eyes and spill over on her cheeks. She hugged Dizz close and buried her face against Dizz's shoulder.

When Dizz could talk again, she poured out her pitiful tale. She had thought Chris was going to run off with Carol, and she had gone to George out of spite. Now she despised him for what had happened.

"I know I've got no right to hold you," Dizz sobbed. "I know you probably hate me. But, Chris, I need you. You said you wouldn't leave me, Chris. You said you wouldn't."

"No, darling," Chris said. "I won't leave you. I don't think I even wanted to." She tilted Dizz's face to hers and kissed her hard on the mouth. "I belong to you, Dizz. I always have."

They clung together like two drowning souls to a straw. After a while they slept.

It was dark when Chris awoke. She moved Dizz and raised her arm to peer at the watch. Nine-thirty. She had to call Carol.

Dizz stirred and rolled away from her. She opened her eyes. "Darling," she said. "Say it again. Say you won't leave me."

"I won't leave you, Dizz," Chris said. "I love you."

They kissed long and tenderly.

Dizz got up and switched on the light. She looked at Chris and laughed. "You look like Barney Google," she said.

"You don't look so good yourself."

Dizz touched the handkerchief on Chris' hand. "We'd better fix that," she said.

"It's all right," Chris said.

"How do you feel, Chris? You look like you had a pretty rough time of it."

"I did," Chris said. "But I'm fine. Just hungry."

Dizz started toward the kitchen. "That's easy to cure," she said.

Chris started after her. "Dizz, wait a minute," she said. "I have to call Carol. She's expecting me tonight."

"My," Dizz said. "You were anxious, weren't you?" She shook her head scoldingly, then smiled. Her eyes were not smiling.

"Look," Chris said. "I'm only calling to settle the matter. You can listen, if you want."

"Honey," Dizz said. "Will you promise me something?"

"What?"

"That you won't see Carol again," Dizz said. "And I promise that I won't see George."

Chris sighed. It was a logical request. Yet she knew in her heart she wanted to see Carol. To see her and hold her and make love to her as she could never do with Dizz.

But at the same time she needed Dizz. Needed her because she was a part of her. And needed her now to go to Tongariva. Not that that was a particularly noble reason, but at least it was true.

"Right," Chris said. "It's a deal."

Dizz went out to the kitchen and Chris picked up the phone. She dialed the Yukon number.

Carol answered on the first ring.

"Darling," Chris said. "I'm not coming tonight. I'm staying with Dizz."

"What happened?" Carol said.

"I just realized that I love her too much to leave her. Whatever it is we have together," she said, remembering Carol's description of the relationship, "I need it."

There was a long silence on the other end of the line. Then Carol said, "I hope you know what you're doing, Chris."

"I do," Chris answered.

She heard the tears in Carol's voice. "Goodbye, darling," Carol said. Then she hung up.

Chris put down the receiver. She felt suddenly very cold and alone, like the fire was gone.

She walked into the kitchen and stood looking at Dizz. Dizz was whistling, like the world was still the same old world. Like tonight and the weekend had never happened.

Dizz turned to smile at Chris. "Ten minutes," she said.

Chris nodded and went to wash up for dinner.

19

The phone woke Chris at five after nine. It was
Jonathan.

"I just got a call from someone in Carol's
building," he said. "She's left town. I just called to
find out if Sheila's become a grass widow."

Chris could see the smirk over the phone.

"No," she answered. "I'm still here. And I aim to
stay." She banged down the receiver. Her first
thought was to say, Damn him. Then she remembered
what he had said. She frowned. It didn't make sense
to her for Carol to have gone.

Dizz was standing in the doorway, stretching sleepily. "What was that?" she said.

"Jonathan," Chris said. "Carol's left town. He was hoping I went with her."

"Why?"

"You," Chris said. "He still thinks he can make out if I drop dead."

Dizz laughed nastily. "That fat poppycock!" She turned back to the bedroom, unbuttoning the pajama top and reaching for a bra.

Chris went into the bathroom and washed the sleep out of her eyes. She looked in the mirror. Her eyes were puffy from crying. Her cheeks were scratched and streaked with iodine. A lovely sight early in the morning.

She remembered Carol kneeling beside her on the beach, kissing her bloody hand. She wondered guiltily where the girl had gone.

It didn't seem right that Carol would walk out on her job like that. She was good at her job and she liked it. Chris did not comprehend how anybody could let a thing like a broken heart ruin his life. She thought of Max Petersen and the filthy apartment and the fat blonde.

She went back into the bedroom and took a pair of slacks out of the closet. She dressed slowly. She knew she should be thinking of Dizz and how to make up to her for the mess of this weekend. Dizz wouldn't show it, but she would be blaming Chris for what had happened. And Chris wanted Dizz to be agreeable for awhile.

But somehow the business of Carol was getting

out of hand. Chris felt responsible and a little ashamed.

Chris managed to get through breakfast. Dizz was in a good mood and making funny. She had had a good night's sleep, apparently, and now had nothing on her conscience. She had cried it all away and it was gone. Chris didn't have the energy to keep up the banter. She left the kitchen and walked out to the terrace.

She sat down on the wooden lawn chair, stretched out and looked up to the sky. It would be raining soon. Maybe if she just sat here long enough, she would wash down the drain with the rest of the dirt; just disappear and not have to think and feel and suffer anymore.

In a second floor window directly across from Chris a woman was getting dressed. She struggled to hook her bra, then slid into a slip. She came to stand at the window and look out, lifting her arms to toss back the long brown hair. She put back her head and smiled. For just a second she reminded Chris of Carol.

Chris threw herself off the chair and went back inside. The sudden jump wrenched her crippled leg and she leaned against the wall in pain.

"Chris, what's wrong?" Dizz said. She was busily dusting the living room. She had an ashtray in her hand and she did not bother to stop.

"I forgot about the leg for a minute," Chris said. "It's still pretty sore."

"Why don't you go soak in the tub?" Dizz said. "It would probably take out some of the stiffness."

Chris went into the bathroom and turned on the hot water in the basin. She didn't feel like getting undressed for a bath but it might help to soak her hands. Her head too, maybe. She dipped her hands into the steaming water and flexed the fingers.

Dizz turned on the sweeper. The shrill whine caught at Chris' nerves and she felt a shiver of irritation run up her spine. She let the water out of the sink, went back to her bedroom and shut the door.

She sat down at the desk and picked up a pencil. She put it down. She pushed some papers into a neater pile. She propped her feet on the desk and folded her arms.

It started to rain, all of a sudden, driving hard. She heard Dizz banging the windows, got up and shut the window in the room. She sat down again.

Dizz was back with the sweeper.

Chris picked up a gum eraser and heaved it at the wall. She watched it bounce and roll under the bed. She did not bother to retrieve it.

Then she got up and went to the closet. She took out a trench coat, and went back to the living room.

Dizz looked up and shut off the machine.

"I have to go out for a while," Chris said.

Dizz looked at her disgustedly. "You're going to be stiff as a board if you go out there," she said. "You'll be drenched."

"I can't help it," Chris said angrily. "I'm giving myself the creeps."

Dizz waved her away. "Go," she said.

Chris left the building and limped painfully

through the rain to the corner of First Avenue. She waited three minutes for a cab, then told the driver to rush it to Seventy-second.

Chris had to keep reminding herself that what she had done to Carol was a rotten thing. It was much simpler to believe that Carol had done her wrong, that Carol didn't understand, just as Dizz never had. How could Carol run out on her without giving her a chance?

Chris remembered Carol's little speech about Dizz and how she could not fight her, how she would not sneak around behind Dizz's back. If she had really meant it, then maybe she had gone away for good.

She was nervous and shaky when she entered Carol's building. Her temples were throbbing and she felt the first flush of fever burn through her. The wetness of the hall and her own hair and clothes clung in her throat. She did not find the smell of the halls nostalgic or appealing. It turned her stomach.

She knocked at Carol's door and waited for a long time. She knocked again. There was no answer. She tried the apartment next door.

A woman with her hair in pin curls and wearing a bathrobe came to the door. She looked up at Chris and the look was not pleasant.

Chris smiled. "I'm a friend of Carol Martin," she said. "I was supposed to meet her here." It was the only dodge she could think of.

"Carol went away," the woman said.

"Oh?" Chris said. "Do you know where?"

"She asked me to call her boss and say she was leaving town is all I know," the woman said. "I saw her downstairs. She asked me to call and she said she wouldn't be back except to move her stuff. She went off with a red-headed guy in a station wagon."

"Thank you," Chris said.

She went back down the stairs, leaning heavily against the bannister. It should have been easier, the trip down. But it was worse.

Why in the hell did she do that? Chris wondered. She's not in love with Johnnie. She's in love with me.

She crossed First Avenue and went into a Greek luncheonette. She was already soaked to the skin through the trench coat. She could feel the wet bandage on her shoulder plastered to her torn flesh.

"Coffee," she said.

She sat nursing the cup. By now she knew beyond doubt that she was ill. Her head was burning and the palms of her hands were clammy. A trickle of perspiration shivered down her back. Her insides were heaving and she had a mild case of the shakes.

But she had more important things on her mind. She was remembering again Carol's lecture on the subject of Dizz. What was it Carol had said? If you're going to live with Dizz, you'll have to stop seeing me.

It had never occurred to Chris for a moment that somehow she couldn't eat her cake and have it too. Of course she wanted Dizz; she needed her. But she wanted Carol, too, and needed her. But she hadn't considered the possibility that she couldn't have them both.

In all the years of her adult life, Chris had never encountered a woman who told her what to do. She'd run through more women than she cared to count. It had been like a game. She'd believed in having a hell

182

of a good time, then just walking away. She had never taken anybody seriously.

Then Dizz came along. The serpent in her Garden of Eden. Dizz had gotten inside her soul and, like a cancer, taken root. Dizz — who had knocked her down and then spent four years kicking her; who had never shown her anything but contempt, never really cared about anything but the dull ache of misery in her own heart.

Then Carol. She had come into Chris' life and started patching up the wounds Dizz had opened. She had been everything good and warm, everything Dizz was not. And now Carol had betrayed her.

It did not occur to Chris at the moment that perhaps Carol had felt betrayed herself. All she could realize was that Carol had walked out on her and that Carol had one hell of a nerve. And Chris intended to find out just what the devil Carol thought she was doing.

Chris gulped the cold coffee and slid off the stool. She walked to the back of the lunchroom and stepped into a phone booth. She put in a long distance call to Johnnie's lodge.

"Yeah, skipper," Johnnie's voice said. "She's here."

"Why, Johnnie?" Chris asked.

Johnnie waited a minute, then said simply, "Skipper, you may never have known this, I guess. But some people don't like being kicked around."

"But I love her, Johnnie," Chris said. She knew she was beginning to sound desperate.

"Look, kid, you promised Carol you'd come live with her, right?"

"Yes," Chris said. "But she knows I have to hang

on to Dizz until after this trip. We could have worked something out then."

"Carol doesn't go for that, skipper," Johnnie said. Chris knew Johnnie had been coached in his lines. "She thinks you'll never leave blondie. She thinks you'd just use her to calm you down, like you use the rest of them."

"She loves me," Chris said.

"Yeah," Johnnie said. "She loves you. Maybe she'll get over it someday. Maybe not. But I'm going to keep an eye on her just in case. She might decide to settle for me. At least, that's what I'm hoping."

Chris left the lunchroom and walked back into the rain. She couldn't help feeling a grudging admiration for Carol — it took courage to give up somebody you love, somebody you know is no damned good for you.

Chris headed toward home. She didn't especially want to go back, but for the moment she couldn't think of anything else to do with herself.

Where's to go but home? What do you do when somebody you love tells you all about yourself? Where can you go but home and stuff your head under a pillow and sob?

With a sudden frightening clarity Chris realized that she would never see Carol again. Until that instant of realization, she hadn't really believed it. It was to her mind like having a little argument and going to bed mad. Tomorrow you would kiss and make up. That's the way it ought to be when you love somebody — kiss and make up.

But she would have no tomorrow with Carol. Not even many yesterdays. Only a little over a week. Just a couple of minutes out of a lifetime, a few minutes of perfect happiness to lock away somewhere and save to enjoy in her old age, when she was too worn to feel it.

Chris felt hot with fever and shame and anger. She had held it, right there in her fingers, and she had let it slip away. Oh, the weak, sniveling fool that she was.

She stopped in the middle of the street and sent a curse home to Dizz. A curse on Dizz for not being what she wanted her to be, for being her own damned self.

But why bother, she thought. It's me, it's me.

Chris decided she could use a drink.

20

Chris sat in the back room of Tony's, cupping a shot glass in her palm. She was on her fourth round. She wanted to get very very drunk, drunk enough to forget. But the liquor didn't touch her.

She leaned her fist on her chin and glared across the room at a bullfight poster on the opposite wall. Under the poster were two long-haired blondes in leotards and trench coats, hunched over a table and gazing deep into each other's eyes, sighing now and then and occasionally touching fingers. They had neither moved nor spoken for an hour. They thought they were in love.

The swinging doors banged open and then shut behind someone. Chris glanced up. It was the fat blonde with the beautiful green eyes. Jennie. She was wearing a tight black dress and no coat, despite the rain. Her hair hung in wet strings.

Jennie spotted Chris and sidled drunkenly across to her table. She looked as though she had never been completely sober in all her life. She pulled out a chair and sat down.

"Hi, big boy," she said. "Who the hell hit you?"

"A truck," Chris said.

"Oh?" Jennie said. "Blonde or brunette?"

"Redhead," Chris answered. She was in no mood for Jennie. She had too much on her mind to bother being charming to a female like this one.

"I've been looking for you, handsome," Jennie said. "Cruising all these crummy bars. Where you been hiding?" She moved close to Chris and pressed a thigh against her.

Chris picked up the shot glass and drained it. "I don't spend much time in the bars," she said.

"You married?" Jennie asked.

"Yeah, I'm married," Chris answered. Some hell of a marriage, but she had always thought of the arrangement with Dizz as that.

"Oh," Jennie said. She put her hand on Chris' leg and moved it slowly upward.

Chris grabbed the wrist and pushed the hand away. She wanted to slap the girl, but hesitated to start what would end up as a brawl.

"I live near here," Jennie said.

Chris sighed. "Look, Jennie," she said. "No dice."

"C'mon, handsome," Jennie said. "She'll keep the bed warm."

Chris smiled to herself at the irony of it.

Chris stood up and pushed back the chair. "No good, kid," she said. "I've got things on my mind." She handed the waiter a ten and told him to keep the change.

She left the bar without looking back, stopped a cab at the corner and got in. She felt almost glad for the incident with Jennie. It was the first time in four years that she had turned down an offer, and that felt good.

When she left the cab, Chris went to stand in the rain and look down at the river. She pressed her face close to the wire of the fence. Somewhere out in the darkness was Carol. Somewhere behind her was Dizz. And somewhere in the middle she stood on an island, clinging to a fence. Too sober, too sad, and too lonely.

She walked back to the house and went in. She could hardly move now. Her body was hot with fever and wracked with pain. She felt sick and tired and very old. She hoped Dizz would be good to her tonight. Or, if she was in a foul mood, just ignore her altogether.

Dizz was squatting on the kitchen floor, waggling a scolding finger. In front of her on the linoleum was a very large puddle and a very small dog. She did not bother to look up when Chris opened the door.

Chris closed the door behind her and walked into the living room. She took off her trench coat and threw it into the sling chair. She kicked off her shoes, pulled off her socks, then took off her shirt and dropped it on top of the trench coat.

When she could talk again, she walked back into the kitchen. Dizz and the pup were still glaring at each other defiantly. The puddle had been wiped up, but the pup had not apologized.

"Where did he come from?" Chris asked quietly.

"George left him," Dizz said. "He has to be out of town for about a week. I said we'd take care of Schnitzel." She made it sound like the most natural thing in the world.

"Did you, now?" Chris said. "I thought you weren't going to be seeing George."

Dizz picked up the puppy and stood up. "I'm not seeing him," she said. "But I didn't see anything wrong with baby sitting for a few days. Are you hungry?"

"No," Chris said. "Just nauseous."

Chris turned and limped into the bathroom. She closed the door behind her and turned on the hot water full blast in the tub. She sat down on the john and dragged herself out of the rest of her clothes. She dropped them on the floor, then ripped off the soaked bandage and flushed it down the toilet.

She turned the water off and climbed in. She leaned back against the tub. The hot water felt good on her aching limbs, but it didn't help where she hurt the most.

Completely depressed now, Chris could see no way out. Maybe she was supposed to spend the rest of her life baking in hot tubs and hobbling around the house; maybe she had no right to expect anything good out of the future. She'd had a chance and she had muffed it. Maybe she would never get another one — maybe she wouldn't know one if she saw it.

Dizz opened the door and came in. She sat down on the john with Schnitzel on her lap.

"Christopher," Dizz said, "this has got to stop." She looked decidedly unhappy.

"What has?" Chris said.

"You," Dizz said. "Moping around in a rage. If there's anything wrong, let's get it over."

Chris looked at her sadly and shook her head. "You just don't understand, do you?" she said. And she knew as she said it that Dizz wouldn't even know what she was talking about.

"Understand what?"

Chris sighed. "Did it ever occur to you, my dear," she said, "that we're supposed to be leaving for Tongariva the day after tomorrow?"

"Oh, Chris, don't be an ass," Dizz said with impatience. "You know very well you can't go diving in the condition you're in now."

Chris flushed angrily. "But you didn't bother to ask about my plans," she said.

Schnitzel stood up on Dizz's lap and turned around. He sat down again and yawned. He propped his rump on Dizz's thigh and buried his nose under her wrist. He kept one eye open, staring at Chris.

"Honey," Dizz said, "if it's so damned important to you, I can get Mother to keep Schnitzel."

Chris sighed. She knew this was getting nowhere fast.

"That's not the point," Chris said.

"What's the point?"

"When did you agree to keep Schnitzel?" Chris

said. She tried hard to keep her voice low. She
wanted to shout at Dizz and make her understand.

Dizz thought for a minute. "I don't know," she
said. "Sometime last week. Why?"

"In other words," Chris said, "you never did
intend to go to Tongariva." She glared at Dizz
accusingly and Dizz averted her eyes.

Dizz hesitated. She looked just slightly
uncomfortable. "Well," she said, "I meant it when I
said it. But I didn't think you'd take it so seriously."

"Oh, never mind," Chris said. She pulled herself
up and climbed out of the tub. She grabbed a towel
and began rubbing. "The point is, I need you now.
Jonathan wants you to be along to keep me out of
trouble. He'll keep me at home if you don't go. And,
Dizz, I want to make this trip."

"All right," Dizz said quietly. "I'll go." She stood
up and held onto Schnitzel.

"Thanks," Chris said bitterly. She wrapped the
towel around her and left the bathroom. She picked
up the clothes in the living room and carried them to
her room.

In pajamas and a bath robe Chris sprawled out on
the bed and propped her bare feet against the wall.
She looked out through the doorway and watched
Dizz playing with Schnitzel on the floor. She caught
herself smiling and knew she was lost. As usual.

There was no help for it, Chris decided. Even
when she was hating Dizz, she was still in love with
her. She looked adorable now with the little pup.
Adorable and beautiful and . . .

Oh, God, what's to become of me, Chris thought.
She's killing me. But I can't give her up. I can't.

Killing me? I'm killing myself. It's not Dizz. It's

me. I can't blame her if I'm a failure. And I can't even blame her if my knees turn to water every time I look at her.

Dizz looked up at her from the living room and smiled that crazy delicious smile.

Chris felt herself slipping. She still wanted that smile. And she still wanted Dizz, for all the frustration of it. What the hell. She couldn't go back to a world full of Jennies.

Chris was really too stiff and sore to move, but she wanted to be near Dizz, to let her know things were all right — that they were right. So she heaved herself off the bed and went into the other room to lower herself painfully to the couch. She stuck out a toe for Schnitzel to chew on.

"Honey," Chris said, "how about some coffee? I'm not feeling very well. I think I've got a fever."

Dizz got up and put a palm on Chris' forehead. "You certainly have," she said. "I think I'd better call the doctor."

"No," Chris said. "Just get the coffee."

Chris picked up Schnitzel and sat playing with him until Dizz came back into the room. Then she put him down and took the cup from Dizz and swallowed a gulp of the hot coffee. She set the cup on the end table.

Dizz came and curled up beside her on the couch. She put her head on Chris' shoulder and kissed her on the cheek.

Chris took Dizz's hand and held it in her lap. She wanted to put an arm around her. But her arms were too sore to lift.

"Darling," Dizz said.

"Hmmm?"

"How much does this trip mean to you?" Dizz asked.

Chris had been expecting this. She knew Dizz did not want to go. And right at the moment she was far too ill to give a good damn. It did not seem important anymore. All that mattered was that they shouldn't argue anymore. That they should just be quiet for a while and then go to sleep.

"Well," Chris said slowly, "yesterday it was a matter of life and death. At the moment, I'm not so sure. Why?"

"It would make me a lot happier," Dizz said, "if you would call it off."

"Why?" Chris said.

"Because I really don't believe you're in any condition to go," she said. "You're bandaged and stiff and now you've got a fever. How about it?"

Chris sat very still. She couldn't argue with Dizz about her physical condition. She felt lousy. If she were dumped in the ocean now, she would sink like a stone.

But she had to consider something else, at least for a second.

What would happen if she backed out? Jonathan would scream, for one thing. He was counting on her to help finance the deal. And he wanted her to be there, whether he admitted it or not. He knew he could trust her to know a Glory-of-the-Seas when she saw one, even if he couldn't trust her to stay out of the water.

But what would happen to her? If she quit now, would she ever have what it would take to go diving again? Or would she spend the rest of her days regretting that she hadn't gone?

193

She would have to take that chance. She would
have to take that chance because she was just too
wretched to think about it anymore.

"Okay, honey," she said tiredly. "I'll tell Jonathan
in the morning that I won't be going. I have to see
him anyhow."

"Good," Dizz said pleasantly. "Now you'd better
get yourself off to bed."

"Right," Chris said. She let go of Dizz's hand, put
out her feet and tried to stand up. Her head was
splitting and the room did a flip in front of her eyes.

She made it to the bedroom door before she
passed out.

21

When Chris awoke, it was well past noon. She lay still in bed, listening to the rain. It was still pouring hard and dripping off the trees.

Gradually she became aware of other sounds and she knew that Dizz was in the kitchen doing something and that Schnitzel was on the floor beside the bed chewing a shoe. And she knew it was Wednesday afternoon and that she had to see Jonathan. And that she was cold and weak and hungry. The fever was gone.

Chris threw back the covers and quietly made a

good effort to sit up. She got halfway, then she fell back on the bed. The second try was a little more effective. Her feet touched the floor.

Schnitzel abandoned the shoe and bounded onto Chris' foot. She felt his tiny tongue massaging her toes. She reached down and scratched the top of his head.

She got up from the bed and went to the closet and opened the door, careful not to make a sound. She dressed as quickly as she could in a warm suit and shirt, then sat down on the bed to put on her shoes.

She saw Schnitzel run to the door. She looked up and straight at Dizz who was standing in the doorway with a heavy tray.

"And just where do you think you're going, young lady?" Dizz said.

"I have to talk to Jonathan," Chris said.

"Oh, no," Dizz said. "If you have to talk to Jonathan, you can use the telephone." She set the tray down on the desk. "I'm under doctor's orders to keep you in bed."

"I feel fine," Chris said. She walked to the door, put a finger under Dizz's chin and tilted her face up. She kissed her on the nose. "And no arguments from you."

Dizz breathed a resigned sigh. "Well, at least eat something."

"Right," Chris said. She moved across to the desk and sat down.

She did not speak again until she had finished eating. Then she turned to Dizz and said, "I should be back in a couple of hours.

"Shall I come with you?" Dizz said.

"No," Chris answered. "You have to baby sit." She reached down and scratched Schnitzel behind the ears.

"Go," Dizz said. She kissed Chris on the cheek.

By the time she reached the museum, Chris had thought of fifty bad ways to break the news to Jonathan. He didn't give her time to use any of them.

"Chris," he said, jumping up as she came into the office. "Thank heaven, you're here."

"What's wrong?" Chris said.

"Plenty," Jonathan said. "I've been trying for two days to get a good diver. All I've been able to come up with is Nevins."

"And what's wrong with Nevins?"

"Nothing's wrong with him," Jonathan said. "It's just that he's used to doing salvage work. He doesn't know the first thing about spotting shells."

Chris understood. She knew it was a matter of knowing where to look, of knowing what you were looking for and being able to recognize it when you found it. She realized that Nevins had no experience along these lines. He knew more about a blow torch than he would ever know about a Glory-of-the-Seas.

It hurt her to say it, but she had promised Dizz.

"Jonathan," she said slowly, "this will break your heart. But I'm not going."

"What?" he screamed.

"Dizz chickened out on me," Chris said. "You said you wanted her to be along."

Jonathan paused for just one second. "Forget about her," he said. "Do you want to go?"

Chris walked to a chair and sat down. "I promised her I wouldn't," Chris said. "She's worried about my

197

physical condition. I keeled over last night. She's afraid I'm not well enough to make the trip."

"Chris," Jonathan said, "that's not what I asked you. I asked you if you want to go."

Chris flushed red. She knew Jonathan was putting her on the spot for a good reason, and that he knew as well as she did that she wanted desperately to make this trip. He understood that behind all her physical misery and the tortured anguish of the past few days was still the old Chris Hamilton who would risk her neck for a good shell any day. And for this particular shell would risk everything she had.

"Yes, Jonathan," Chris said. "You know damned well I want to go. But —"

"But you promised Sheila," Jonathan said. "Look, Chris. This could be the chance of a lifetime for you." He looked at her pleadingly. "You said so yourself."

"Yes," she said, "I know. It could also mean disaster for you if I don't go."

"That's true," he admitted. "The Board of Directors would hardly approve of my having spent a small fortune on something that turned out to be a total flop."

Chris ran her fingers through her hair. She stood up and walked to the window. She walked back. She looked at Jonathan and shook her head sadly.

"Jonathan," she said, "I'm truly sorry. But I can't."

He sighed. "At least think it over, will you?"

"I'll think it over," she said.

She left Jonathan without saying goodbye.

In the middle room a young man with sandy hair, wearing dirty white bucks and a bright red tie, was busily fussing over a new display. On a twelve-foot table had been laid out a detailed relief map of the Florida Keys, finished in sand-crusted plaster of Paris and sea blue silk. Tidily arranged in the appropriate spots were the best of the specimens Chris had picked up on her last trip. A small white card, meticulously lettered in Carol's fine print, identified each shell. Chris spotted the "Hamilton" in the bottom right corner of each card.

When she had carefully circled the table twice, Chris turned to the young man and said, "That's quite an impressive lay-out."

The young man blinked at her owlishly through thick black-framed lenses.

"I'd like to make one correction though, if I may."

"Well," the young man hesitated, "I don't know, ma'am. I'm not supposed to let anybody touch it till Dr. Brandt says it's all right."

Chris smiled. "It's okay," she said. "I'm Chris Hamilton. I brought these shells in."

"Oh, Miss Hamilton," he said breathlessly, "I'm sorry, I didn't recognize you."

"Forget it," Chris said. "There's no reason why you should have."

She moved along one side of the table. "This," she said, moving a tiny cone shell about three inches and setting it down, "belongs over here." She picked up the marker and put it down by the shell. She stepped back and surveyed the table. "That's better," she said.

"Thanks, Miss Hamilton," the young man said. "I'm Tommy Samson. I just started this morning."

"I'm glad to know you, Tommy," Chris said.

199

"Miss Hamilton," Tommy said slowly, "I've seen the collection of treasure maps they've got upstairs. All the ones you brought in, I mean."

"Yes?" Chris said.

"Well," he went on, "I've got about fifty old maps that I'm pretty proud of. I picked them up in book stores and second hand shops. I was wondering if maybe you would take a look at them sometime. I don't know if they're worth anything or not, but I'm sure you'd know."

Chris smiled. "I'd be glad to look at them, Tommy. I hope I'll be able to tell you what you want to know."

As she limped into the solarium, Chris was thinking about Tommy and his maps. She chuckled wryly to herself. She could see herself ten years from now, sitting in an arm chair by the fire, giving the final authority on maps and travelogues and the like.

But, damn it, she thought, I didn't pick mine up in book shops. I went out and found them. In Singapore and in Cuba and in a pawn shop in Paris. And I never spent my time setting up displays in a museum either. I went diving for those shells. In every puddle of water big enough to hold me. It's all wrong somehow.

The solarium had changed. Tommy had moved in. A striped chino jacket hung on the back of a chair. A container of orange juice sat where the coffee belonged. There were no signs left of Carol.

Chris sighed. She sat down at the desk and propped her foot on the other chair. She opened the middle drawer and took out the blue drawing pencil. She held it lightly between two fingers and drummed it against the desk.

Dizz, old girl, she thought, you and I are going to have a nice long talk this evening.

Talk about what, Chris? Dizz'll take one look at you and laugh in your face. And she's right. You're so beat up now you can hardly walk. And just what do you think will happen to you if you try to dive now? You'd better save that for the bathtub, old girl.

But, Dizz, you don't understand. Bathtubs are for baths. I'm not ready to retire yet. I'm not ready to die, Dizz. Sure I'm scared. I'm scared as hell, all over again. I know now what it feels like to be trapped under water and look death straight in the eye. And I know the prettiest sound in the world is the surf on the beach because when you hear it you know you won't drown.

In fact, I was so damned scared and so damned tired that I almost let you convince me that I belonged in dry dock. Almost, Dizz. I let you look at me and smile that crazy smile and hypnotize me like you always do. What for? Oh, no, Dizz darling, not because you're worried about me or what might happen to me. You never worried about anything in your life but good old Dizz. But because you don't like water and sand and sea shells.

Chris bit down hard on the end of the pencil. Maybe she wasn't being fair. Too harsh, maybe. Maybe Dizz really did care what happened to her.

She wondered for the ten millionth time if Dizz loved her. Not that it really mattered. The way she hung onto Dizz was her own sickness, her own pet form of masochism. It had very little to do with love.

Carol had known that. That's why she had pulled out. She'd had sense and strength enough not to get caught in this destructive web.

Chris put her face in her hands and wept without tears. She was feeling terribly, terribly sorry for herself. She felt as though she were running circles around herself. Muddled, muddled brain.

Chris knew that the confusion had started with Carol. Before that she had been miserable, but she had been able to live with it. In just one week, Carol had shown her what it was like to be loved and appreciated, what it was like to share love with somebody. And Carol had made her take a good look at this shabby thing she had with Dizz.

Carol had done everything, in fact, except tell her how — how to pick up and walk out on something that you've thought was your whole life.

Somewhere way in the back of her mind, Chris felt a fact demanding indignantly to be heard. The very simple fact that though Carol had not told her, she had shown her how to do it.

Chris felt a hand on her shoulder.

"Is anything wrong, Miss Hamilton?" Tommy asked. His voice was worried.

Chris looked up. "No," she smiled. "Nothing's wrong." No, Tommy, nothing at all.

Chris stood up tiredly and moved away from the desk. "Bring the maps in any time," she said.

Tommy grinned. "Thanks," he said.

He watched her hobble out of the room and shook his head sadly.

Chris did not see him, but she felt it. And she cringed. To that boy, Chris thought, I must look like a hundred and ten and finished. Sad, he's thinking, to lose Miss Hamilton. She was good in her day.

Chris stood up straight and stopped limping.

It's about time, she decided, for Miss Hamilton to stop feeling sorry for herself.

22

Chris entered the apartment full of the determination to blast Dizz off the face of the earth, if necessary. She'd be as gentle as she possibly could, but Dizz or no Dizz, Chris Hamilton was going to be on that plane to Tongariva tomorrow morning.

She had her mouth open to make the announcement as she came through the doorway. She didn't get the chance. Dizz was not there.

Chris swore bitterly to herself. Only she knew

what it had cost her to work up enough nerve to assert herself with Dizz. And she wasn't at all sure it would last.

She walked into the living room and turned on the lamp at the end of the couch. She took off her shoes and kicked them under a chair, then went to the liquor cabinet and fixed herself a stiff drink from a half empty bottle of scotch. She drank it down quickly and poured another.

She looked at the mail Dizz had left on top of the cabinet. A brown envelope with a telephone bill and an ad for vitamin tablets. She didn't bother to look at the bill and dropped the ad into the waste paper basket.

She went into the kitchen and set the drink on the table. It left a ring of liquid on the polished surface. She took the sponge from the sink, wiped the table and dried the bottom of the glass. She put the drink on the stove and threw the sponge into the sink.

The well-trained spouse, she thought. She wrinkled her nose distastefully.

She opened the refrigerator. She was confronted as usual by neat packages of heaven knew what in aluminum foil. She hated the dullness of it.

She slammed the refrigerator door and turned to the cupboard. A box of crackers, soup, cranberry sauce, more soup, sardines. She took down the can of sardines and stuck it into the opener. She cranked the handle, then took the can on her palm and reached for a fork.

She ate standing up. She drained the glass. Then

she dumped soap powder on the fork and scrubbed it hard to get off the fishy smell. She rinsed out the glass. She wrung the water out of the sponge.

She sighed.

She went back to the living room and sprawled out on the couch. She closed her eyes, hoping maybe she'd doze off and relax a little, get some of the ache out of that blasted leg and the shakes out of her body.

But she could not sleep. Her ears were straining toward the door, listening for Dizz. She figured Dizz ought to be back soon. She was probably just out doing some shopping, or walking Schnitzel.

She wanted a cigarette. Really wanted one.

A drop of water splashed into the sink. A branch creaked outside the French windows. Somebody upstairs flushed a john. Nobody came in the front door.

Chris lay on the couch listening and wanting a cigarette. Every ten minutes she looked at her watch.

The phone rang at ten minutes and twenty seconds after eight. It was Dizz.

"Chris," Dizz said. "I'm at Mother's. I've decided to stay over."

Chris made a nasty face, but said nothing.

"Chris? What's the matter?"

"I wanted to talk to you," Chris said. "I've been thinking about this Tongariva deal and —"

"It'll wait till morning," Dizz said impatiently. "I'll be back early."

"But —"

"I can't talk now," Dizz said.

Chris hung up the receiver.

It'll wait till morning. You'll wait till morning,

Chris. You'll wait until I have time to get around to you. You'll wait, Chris.

Chris went into her bedroom and took a pack of cigarettes out of the dresser. She took the lighter out of a jacket pocket. It was dry. She found some matches in the desk. She went back to the couch.

She finished the third cigarette before she decided to get really angry. Then she fumed. Here she was, tired and sick and needing somebody to take care of her. She had been sick enough to need a doctor last night. And she really didn't feel at all well now. And the person who was supposed to be catering to her, where was she? At Mother's. And Dizz hadn't even bothered to ask how she felt.

The pack of cigarettes was empty before she fell asleep. So was the bottle of scotch.

Her watch showed nine-thirty when the buzzer rang. Chris shook herself awake and got up and went to the kitchen to push the button.

She opened the door.

Dizz entered and walked straight to her bedroom. Schnitzel was not with her.

Chris closed the door and followed Dizz into the room. She was too furious to trust herself to speak.

Dizz was lying on her back on the bed, staring at the ceiling. She did not look at Chris.

Chris sat down on a chair to wait. She made herself comfortable, knowing from experience it might be a long time. This was one of Dizz's favorite poses.

When she could sit still no longer, Chris asked quietly, "What happened this time?"

"Nothing," Dizz said dully. She did not move. She did not bother to look at Chris.

Chris got up and went to stand beside the bed.

"Look," she said, "this may sound indelicate of me. But I don't have time for a tantrum this morning. Sit up."

Still Dizz did not move.

Chris put out her hand and grabbed the lapels of Dizz's coat. She pulled her into a sitting position. "I said sit up," she said between her teeth. She pulled the coat tight in her fist and shook Dizz hard.

Dizz looked at her and straight through.

"Where's Schnitzel?" Chris said.

"With George," Dizz said.

"That's what I figured," Chris said. "You'd better have a good story, kid."

Dizz was still looking through her. "He got back early," Dizz said. "He came for Schnitzel."

"And?" Chris said.

"That's all," Dizz said.

"You're lying, Dizz."

Dizz focused. The look was full of hate. "What do you want from me?" she said.

"The truth," Chris said. "If you know how."

"All right," Dizz said. The deep voice was flat and dead. "I knew he'd be back yesterday. I'd promised to see him. He knew how upset I was after that weekend. He wanted a chance to make friends again." There was no expression in her eyes or on her face.

"And you spent another night with him, after the way you felt the other day?" Chris said wonderingly.

"Yes," Dizz said. "I thought I was in love with him. I even thought so after this weekend. I thought we could work out this sex problem."

Chris laughed. "Like we have," she said. "Anyway, are you?"

"What?"

"In love with him," Chris said.

"No," Dizz said.

"That's too bad," Chris said. She let go of Dizz's coat, pushing the girl away from her in disgust, and stood up.

"What do you mean?" Dizz said.

"Never mind," Chris said. She sat down in the chair. She sat back and crossed her legs, coldly self-possessed. "I'm curious," she said. "Why did you bother promising me you wouldn't see George again?"

"I wasn't sure I would."

"You're contradicting yourself, Dizz," Chris said. "You just said —"

"You were yelling at me," Dizz said. "What did you expect me to say?"

Chris shook her head. "No, Dizz," she said. "That won't do at all. You said that to make me get rid of Carol. It wasn't necessary. It will probably please you to know that she dumped me instead."

"Why?" Dizz said.

"Because she thought I was wrapped so tight around your finger that I'd never be able to break loose," Chris said. "And she was almost right."

For a moment Chris felt a wave of depression. She had lost Carol in vain. But maybe not in vain. Without Carol she would never have been able to free herself of Dizz.

Dizz looked at her sharply. "What's the matter with you?" she said.

"Absolutely nothing," Chris said.

Dizz moved to the edge of the bed and sat watching Chris closely.

"Dizz, my loyal spouse," Chris said mockingly, "tell me a couple of other things. Why did you talk me out of going to Tongariva?"

"Because you'd been hurt, of course."

"Don't lie to me, Dizz," Chris said quietly, "or I'll break your goddamned neck. You didn't care enough about me to stay home and take care of me. Or even to ask how I felt."

Dizz knew better than to quibble with the anger on Chris' face. "Jonathan called and told me about the deal he'd made with you. I didn't want to go. I — I had to find out how I felt about George."

Chris nodded. "That sounds reasonable," she said. "I can go to hell so long as you find out about George. Or whatever else you've got a thing for at the moment."

Dizz started to protest.

"Ah ah ah," Chris said, raising a warning finger. "I haven't got time to listen this morning. I have to catch a plane. Now," she said, "just one more little thing. How much money have you got in the bank?"

"About a thousand," Dizz said.

"Good," Chris said. "That should hold you until you find a job. Or another sucker to support you."

"Chris," Dizz cried, "what are you saying?" She slid off the bed and fell on her knees at Chris' feet. "You promised me you wouldn't leave me."

"You should junk that word, kid," Chris said. "It's been kicked around till it's dirty."

"Chris, Chris," Dizz wept, the tears streaming down her face, "I love you."

Chris snorted. "You should have thought of that a long time ago. Before you went after George. Before you decided to give him what you could never give me. You don't know the meaning of love."

"Chris, why are you so angry with me?" Dizz said. Her eyes were miserable and her adorable mouth drawn in pain. The ridiculous smile was forlornly out of place.

"Angry?" Chris said. "I'm not angry, Dizz. Just sick. Sick in my heart and soul. And genuinely sorry." She stood up and stepped away from Dizz. "If I were only angry, I would beat you. To death, probably. But that wouldn't solve anything, now would it?"

Dizz grabbed Chris' leg. "Don't leave me, Chris. Don't leave me. I'll kill myself if you do."

For one second Chris wavered. Then she smiled. She leaned over and lifted Dizz to her feet. She tilted the girl's face up and kissed her tenderly on the lips. "No," she said. "You won't kill yourself, Dizz. Even in my rashest moments, I wouldn't fall for that."

"Chris —"

"Tell you what you do," Chris said. "Just remind yourself that I'm off on a trip. You won't even miss me. I'm sure you never did before."

"But you won't be back?" Dizz said.

"No," Chris said, "I won't be back."

Chris walked out to the living room. Behind her she heard Dizz throw herself on the bed, sobbing bitterly. She closed her ears to the sound.

Chris looked at her watch. Five of eleven. There was still time.

She picked up the phone and dialed the museum.

"Jonathan," she said. "Hold that car. I'll be there in ten minutes. Alone."

A few of the publications of
THE NAIAD PRESS, INC.
P.O. Box 10543 ● Tallahassee, Florida 32302
Phone (904) 539-5965
Mail orders welcome. Please include 15% postage.

CHRIS by Randy Salem. 224 pp. Golden oldie. Handsome Chris
and her adventures. ISBN 0-941483-42-8 $8.95

THREE WOMEN by Sally Singer. 232 pp. Golden oldie. A
triangle among wealthy sophisticates. ISBN 0-941483-43-6   8.95

RICE AND BEANS by Valeria Taylor. 232 pp. Love and
romance on poverty row. ISBN 0-941483-41-X   8.95

PLEASURES by Robbi Sommers. 204 pp. Unprecedented
eroticism. ISBN 0-941483-49-5   8.95

EDGEWISE by Camarin Grae. 372 pp. Spellbinding
adventure. ISBN 0-941483-19-3   9.95

FATAL REUNION by Claire McNab. 216 pp. 2nd Det. Inspec.
Carol Ashton mystery. ISBN 0-941483-40-1   8.95

KEEP TO ME STRANGER by Sarah Aldridge. 372 pp. Romance
set in a department store dynasty. ISBN 0-941483-38-X   9.95

HEARTSCAPE by Sue Gambill. 204 pp. American lesbian in
Portugal. ISBN 0-941483-33-9   8.95

IN THE BLOOD by Lauren Wright Douglas. 252 pp. Lesbian
science fiction adventure fantasy ISBN 0-941483-22-3   8.95

THE BEE'S KISS by Shirley Verel. 216 pp. Delicate, delicious
romance. ISBN 0-941483-36-3   8.95

RAGING MOTHER MOUNTAIN by Pat Emmerson. 264 pp.
Furosa Firechild's adventures in Wonderland. ISBN 0-941483-35-5   8.95

IN EVERY PORT by Karin Kallmaker. 228 pp. Jessica's sexy,
adventuresome travels. ISBN 0-941483-37-7   8.95

OF LOVE AND GLORY by Evelyn Kennedy. 192 pp. Exciting
WWII romance. ISBN 0-941483-32-0   8.95

CLICKING STONES by Nancy Tyler Glenn. 288 pp. Love
transcending time. ISBN 0-941483-31-2   8.95

SURVIVING SISTERS by Gail Pass. 252 pp. Powerful love
story. ISBN 0-941483-16-9   8.95

SOUTH OF THE LINE by Catherine Ennis. 216 pp. Civil War
adventure. ISBN 0-941483-29-0   8.95

WOMAN PLUS WOMAN by Dolores Klaich. 300 pp. Supurb
Lesbian overview. ISBN 0-941483-28-2   9.95

SLOW DANCING AT MISS POLLY'S by Sheila Ortiz Taylor.
96 pp. Lesbian Poetry ISBN 0-941483-30-4   7.95

DREAMS AND SWORDS by Katherine V. Forrest. 192 pp.
Romantic, erotic, imaginative stories.   ISBN 0-941483-03-7   8.95

MEMORY BOARD by Jane Rule. 336 pp. Memorable novel
about an aging Lesbian couple.   ISBN 0-941483-02-9   8.95

THE ALWAYS ANONYMOUS BEAST by Lauren Wright
Douglas. 224 pp. A Caitlin Reese mystery. First in a series.
                                           ISBN 0-941483-04-5   8.95

SEARCHING FOR SPRING by Patricia A. Murphy. 224 pp.
Novel about the recovery of love.   ISBN 0-941483-00-2   8.95

DUSTY'S QUEEN OF HEARTS DINER by Lee Lynch. 240 pp.
Romantic blue-collar novel.   ISBN 0-941483-01-0   8.95

PARENTS MATTER by Ann Muller. 240 pp. Parents'
relationships with Lesbian daughters and gay sons.
                                           ISBN 0-930044-91-6   9.95

THE PEARLS by Shelley Smith. 176 pp. Passion and fun in
the Caribbean sun.   ISBN 0-930044-93-2   7.95

MAGDALENA by Sarah Aldridge. 352 pp. Epic Lesbian novel
set on three continents.   ISBN 0-930044-99-1   8.95

THE BLACK AND WHITE OF IT by Ann Allen Shockley.
144 pp. Short stories.   ISBN 0-930044-96-7   7.95

SAY JESUS AND COME TO ME by Ann Allen Shockley. 288
pp. Contemporary romance.   ISBN 0-930044-98-3   8.95

LOVING HER by Ann Allen Shockley. 192 pp. Romantic love
story.   ISBN 0-930044-97-5   7.95

MURDER AT THE NIGHTWOOD BAR by Katherine V.
Forrest. 240 pp. A Kate Delafield mystery. Second in a series.
                                           ISBN 0-930044-92-4   8.95

ZOE'S BOOK by Gail Pass. 224 pp. Passionate, obsessive love
story.   ISBN 0-930044-95-9   7.95

WINGED DANCER by Camarin Grae. 228 pp. Erotic Lesbian
adventure story.   ISBN 0-930044-88-6   8.95

PAZ by Camarin Grae. 336 pp. Romantic Lesbian adventurer
with the power to change the world.   ISBN 0-930044-89-4   8.95

SOUL SNATCHER by Camarin Grae. 224 pp. A puzzle, an
adventure, a mystery — Lesbian romance.   ISBN 0-930044-90-8   8.95

THE LOVE OF GOOD WOMEN by Isabel Miller. 224 pp.
Long-awaited new novel by the author of the beloved *Patience
and Sarah.*   ISBN 0-930044-81-9   8.95

THE HOUSE AT PELHAM FALLS by Brenda Weathers. 240
pp. Suspenseful Lesbian ghost story.   ISBN 0-930044-79-7   7.95

HOME IN YOUR HANDS by Lee Lynch. 240 pp. More stories
from the author of *Old Dyke Tales.*   ISBN 0-930044-80-0   7.95

EACH HAND A MAP by Anita Skeen. 112 pp. Real-life poems
that touch us all.   ISBN 0-930044-82-7   6.95

SURPLUS by Sylvia Stevenson. 342 pp. A classic early Lesbian
novel.   ISBN 0-930044-78-9   7.95

PEMBROKE PARK by Michelle Martin. 256 pp. Derring-do
and daring romance in Regency England.   ISBN 0-930044-77-0   7.95

THE LONG TRAIL by Penny Hayes. 248 pp. Vivid adventures
of two women in love in the old west.   ISBN 0-930044-76-2   8.95

HORIZON OF THE HEART by Shelley Smith. 192 pp. Hot
romance in summertime New England.   ISBN 0-930044-75-4   7.95

AN EMERGENCE OF GREEN by Katherine V. Forrest. 288
pp. Powerful novel of sexual discovery.   ISBN 0-930044-69-X   8.95

THE LESBIAN PERIODICALS INDEX edited by Claire
Potter. 432 pp. Author & subject index.   ISBN 0-930044-74-6   29.95

DESERT OF THE HEART by Jane Rule. 224 pp. A classic;
basis for the movie *Desert Hearts*.   ISBN 0-930044-73-8   7.95

SPRING FORWARD/FALL BACK by Sheila Ortiz Taylor.
288 pp. Literary novel of timeless love.   ISBN 0-930044-70-3   7.95

FOR KEEPS by Elisabeth Nonas. 144 pp. Contemporary novel
about losing and finding love.   ISBN 0-930044-71-1   7.95

TORCHLIGHT TO VALHALLA by Gale Wilhelm. 128 pp.
Classic novel by a great Lesbian writer.   ISBN 0-930044-68-1   7.95

LESBIAN NUNS: BREAKING SILENCE edited by Rosemary
Curb and Nancy Manahan. 432 pp. Unprecedented autobiographies
of religious life.   ISBN 0-930044-62-2   9.95

THE SWASHBUCKLER by Lee Lynch. 288 pp. Colorful novel
set in Greenwich Village in the sixties.   ISBN 0-930044-66-5   8.95

MISFORTUNE'S FRIEND by Sarah Aldridge. 320 pp. Histori-
cal Lesbian novel set on two continents.   ISBN 0-930044-67-3   7.95

A STUDIO OF ONE'S OWN by Ann Stokes. Edited by
Dolores Klaich. 128 pp. Autobiography.   ISBN 0-930044-64-9   7.95

SEX VARIANT WOMEN IN LITERATURE by Jeannette
Howard Foster. 448 pp. Literary history.   ISBN 0-930044-65-7   8.95

A HOT-EYED MODERATE by Jane Rule. 252 pp. Hard-hitting
essays on gay life; writing; art.   ISBN 0-930044-57-6   7.95

INLAND PASSAGE AND OTHER STORIES by Jane Rule.
288 pp. Wide-ranging new collection.   ISBN 0-930044-56-8   7.95

WE TOO ARE DRIFTING by Gale Wilhelm. 128 pp. Timeless
Lesbian novel, a masterpiece.   ISBN 0-930044-61-4   6.95

AMATEUR CITY by Katherine V. Forrest. 224 pp. A Kate
Delafield mystery. First in a series.   ISBN 0-930044-55-X   7.95

BLACK LESBIANS: AN ANNOTATED BIBLIOGRAPHY
compiled by J. R. Roberts. Foreword by Barbara Smith. 112 pp.
Award-winning bibliography.   ISBN 0-930044-21-5   5.95

THE MARQUISE AND THE NOVICE by Victoria Ramstetter.
108 pp. A Lesbian Gothic novel.   ISBN 0-930044-16-9   6.95

OUTLANDER by Jane Rule. 207 pp. Short stories and essays
by one of our finest writers.   ISBN 0-930044-17-7   8.95

ALL TRUE LOVERS by Sarah Aldridge. 292 pp. Romantic
novel set in the 1930s and 1940s.   ISBN 0-930044-10-X   7.95

A WOMAN APPEARED TO ME by Renee Vivien. 65 pp. A
classic; translated by Jeannette H. Foster.   ISBN 0-930044-06-1   5.00

CYTHEREA'S BREATH by Sarah Aldridge. 240 pp. Romantic
novel about women's entrance into medicine.
                                           ISBN 0-930044-02-9   6.95

TOTTIE by Sarah Aldridge. 181 pp. Lesbian romance in the
turmoil of the sixties.   ISBN 0-930044-01-0   6.95

THE LATECOMER by Sarah Aldridge. 107 pp. A delicate love
story.   ISBN 0-930044-00-2   6.95

ODD GIRL OUT by Ann Bannon.   ISBN 0-930044-83-5   5.95

I AM A WOMAN by Ann Bannon.   ISBN 0-930044-84-3   5.95

WOMEN IN THE SHADOWS by Ann Bannon.
                                           ISBN 0-930044-85-1   5.95

JOURNEY TO A WOMAN by Ann Bannon.
                                           ISBN 0-930044-86-X   5.95

BEEBO BRINKER by Ann Bannon.   ISBN 0-930044-87-8   5.95
              Legendary novels written in the fifties and sixties,
                 set in the gay mecca of Greenwich Village.

VOLUTE BOOKS

JOURNEY TO FULFILLMENT	Early classics by Valerie	3.95
A WORLD WITHOUT MEN	Taylor: The Erika Frohmann	3.95
RETURN TO LESBOS	series.	3.95

These are just a few of the many Naiad Press titles — we are the oldest and
largest lesbian/feminist publishing company in the world. Please request a
complete catalog. We offer personal service; we encourage and welcome
direct mail orders from individuals who have limited access to bookstores
carrying our publications.